BOSSY PLAYBOY

ALEX WOLF
SLOANE HOWELL

Policy: Don't sleep with your brother's secretary.

Problem: Deacon Collins is a wealthy playboy and does what he pleases.

It started out innocent.

He yanked her into the supply closet and lost his briefs. Not the legal kind.

Now, he wants more.

More of her soft curves and sweet mouth.

More than just quickies against a cabinet.

Quinn can throw the flowers he sends in the trash and hide behind company policy all she wants.

At the end of the day...

He *will* have her.

QUINN

WHEN I FIRST TOOK A JOB AT a law firm, I never thought I'd end up in a supply closet with a partner balls-deep inside me.

Oh, and it's not just any partner seconds away from curling my toes—it's Deacon Collins. My boss's brother.

The shameful part is, it's not the first time.

Not even close.

I need to put a stop to it. These quickies are becoming more and more frequent, and I tell myself it's the last after each one.

"Fuck, Quinn." His tone is raspy as his lips drag down the side of my neck. He's possessive and hungry, nipping his teeth along my collarbone as he thrusts into me from behind.

A large, firm hand slides up my thigh and yanks my white panties farther across my ass. I wore them for him. There's something about white seeming virginal that turns him on. I shouldn't encourage his fantasies, but I do. We're playing a dangerous game, sneaking around in a place

1

where we could easily be caught. I think that's part of the thrill for both of us.

I inhale a breath, taking in his masculine scent. There's something primal and raw about Deacon Collins.

He slides out of me, and I immediately miss the connection.

My skirt rides farther up my ass as he turns me and lifts me onto the counter. I wrap my legs around his waist and smirk over his shoulder when I spot new storage containers in the corner. They're filled with everything that once occupied the space where I'm sitting. "Clean up for me?"

"Shit was always in my way." His breath fans over my lips as he leans in closer to kiss me.

He gazes at me with gray eyes that remind me of a storm approaching. His torturous fingers rub over my clit, and I don't know how much more I can take. Deacon loves to toy with me—tease me. He always needs to be in complete control.

His favorite thing to do is bring me to the edge of release then yank me back, over and over.

"Gonna come for me, my dirty little office slut?"

I roll my eyes at him, pretending to be annoyed, but my body betrays me, trembling under his touch. Truth is I would kick his smirking ass if he said anything like that to me anywhere else. But when he's buried inside me, there's something about it that drives me insane.

"Less talking, please."

"Keep mouthing off and I won't let you come at all."

"I can get myself off."

Deacon shakes his head and slides a hand up until it's wrapped around my throat.

My eyes widen.

Deacon smirks. "Not like I can."

I can't argue with him, because he's telling the truth.

Right when I start to mouth something back at him, he shoves in deep and hits my spot just right. I have no earthly clue how this man knows how to push my buttons the way he does.

My walls squeeze around him, craving more. I squirm on the counter, a slave to his touch.

Grabbing a fistful of my hair with his free hand, he growls his words. "Not running that mouth, now. Are you?"

"You like my mouth when your dick's in it."

His eyes roll back for a second, then land on mine. "Fuck, woman."

"That's what you need to do, because we're almost out of time."

The cocky bastard slips out of me, yanks my panties down, drops to his knees, and pushes my legs farther apart. I know he does it just because I told him to hurry.

Deacon moves in, flicking his wicked tongue across my clit. "I'll fuck you when I'm damn good and ready."

I rake my nails through his hair. His confidence is off-the-charts hot, but he needs to take care of business. People will come looking for us soon.

Finally, after teasing me for what seems like an eternity, Deacon lines up with my entrance.

My fingernails bite into his sculpted ass as he slides the head over my clit.

"This what you want?" He grins down at me and eases in.

My eyes roll back. When I'm with Deacon all my worries seem to fade away. Maybe it's why I continue to do this—have sex with him in random places around the office. He gives me an escape I can't get anywhere else. Believe me, I've tried.

I've never been this girl. The girl who wears tight skirts because she knows it turns a man on, but I morph into a different person around him.

His thighs smack into my ass. "If you're staring off into space, I'm not fucking you right."

"No, you're perfect. Don't stop." I gasp when he draws out and slams back in harder.

Gripping my hips, Deacon increases the tempo until my mind is nothing but a blur. Thrusting in and out harder and faster, he clearly has his own agenda now, and I happily race him to the finish line. My head bounces off the cabinet behind me, but I don't care. I ride the wave of pleasure coursing through my body.

His stormy eyes sear into me. His stare feels way too intimate for our relationship. Well, our hooking up. I wouldn't call what we have a relationship.

I like his dick, and he's willing to use it on my terms. No strings attached. We both get what we want—the satisfaction of getting off.

I clench around him and a spasm hits me. Deacon's lips find mine and he grunts against them as he comes. We both jolt a few more times—he groans, I moan his name.

Eventually, we're both reduced to nothing but rough pants and smiles.

"Fuck, that was fantastic."

I put a hand on each of his shoulders and push him off me. "Fun's over."

Stepping back, he removes the condom, shoves it in his pocket, and pulls his pants up.

"Gross, Deacon, you're going to ruin your suit." My nose wrinkles.

"Should I carry it out of here in my fingertips?" He shakes his head at me, laughing.

Fair point.

I hop off the counter and pull my skirt down then hold my hand out. "Panties?"

He waggles his eyebrows. "Finders keepers."

I roll my eyes and smooth my hands over my hair. I don't know what his obsession is with my underwear.

"Let's grab dinner tonight."

I freeze. What did he just say? "Like a date?" I snicker. "You *must* be joking."

"Why's that funny?" His brows draw inward as if my words have wounded him.

What the hell?

"Come on, Deacon. We know what this is."

"What's wrong with going on a date with me?"

I exhale a sigh. "Where should I start? You're a player. We both agreed this was casual. Please don't get weird about this. It's fine the way it is."

"Can't two friends share a meal?"

"We're not friends."

Take the hint, sir!

He shrugs. "Colleagues share meals."

"Enough, Deacon." I need this conversation to end.

5

"It's against company policy. You have a meeting to get to."

Deacon takes one of my hands in his and he looks more determined than I've ever seen him. "I'm not giving up on this. It *will* happen."

I shake my head. He'll grow tired of me soon enough and move on to the next girl. It's what he does.

He stuffs his shirt back into his pants and adjusts his Hugo Boss jacket.

Reaching out, his fingers stroke my cheek. "You're flushed."

I suck in a deep breath and fight the urge to lean into his hand. There's just something that feels natural about it, but I know better. The man is anything but an adult. There's no way he could handle an actual relationship. He takes nothing seriously. I'm not foolish enough to believe I could be the exception.

With a parting smile he slips through the door quietly, taking what seems like all the air with him.

I inhale a few deep breaths to calm myself. There's too much at stake for me to catch feelings for Deacon Collins. I grab a few pens, Wite-Out, and a pad of legal paper so it looks like I have a legitimate reason for being in here.

My eyes flick back and forth as I walk out. Nobody is around, thank God. The last thing I need is to become the hot gossip item at the office.

I place the stuff from the closet in the bottom drawer of my desk. Deacon exits the bathroom and struts past me wearing a smile so big it might get stuck to his smug face.

"Back to work, slacker."

I scowl at him. *Jerk.*

When he reaches his office, I promise myself I won't give him the satisfaction of catching me staring in his direction.

The heat of his gaze burns into my head, though. I lift my eyes, ever so subtly in his direction, and the bastard winks right at me.

Damn it!

I really need to end this.

DEACON

STEPPING off the elevator after a meeting, I spy Quinn behind her desk. She can play this little game all she wants, in fact, it wouldn't be much fun if she didn't.

We both know how it'll end. Honestly, I thought today would be the day she finally caved and said yes. We've snuck around the office a few months now, fucking like rabbits. The first time it happened she swore it was a moment of weakness, a one-time thing, but now look at us.

I pull her into the supply closet a few times a week, and sometimes even on the roof deck. Ahh, the roof deck. There's nothing better than staring out at Lake Michigan while she squeezes that tight pussy around me. My cock hardens at the memories.

Good times. Great oldies.

I continue past her desk, trail a few fingers along the edge, and knock some papers to the floor, just so I can watch her bend over and pick them up.

We both know she's not wearing panties. They're still tucked away in my pocket.

Part of me respects her reluctance. I know my reputation; everyone does. I never date. Dexter calls me a serial monogamist. According to *Chicago Magazine*, I'm one of the city's most eligible bachelors.

Thinking about that, I realize I'm quite a catch. Quinn should be thrilled at the thought of a relationship with me. There are a lot of single women in this city who would kill for an opportunity to go on a date with yours truly.

Thing is, I've never felt this way about a woman before.

It should bug the shit out of me, but it doesn't. I want to get to know Quinn on a deeper level than just physical. Maybe it's just the challenge. The fact she doesn't give in easily. She confuses the hell out of me, strutting around here in skirts, knowing what her tight little ass and those fucking heels do to me.

I damn near have to bite my knuckle to relieve myself of the thought.

The woman is my damn kryptonite. If I want to be taken seriously, I'm going to need a better plan than fucking her into submission. That much is clear.

I stop just inside my office to enjoy the view.

Right when I'm about to get a nice little show from Quinn, Tate Reynolds comes out of nowhere. "I got it." She bends down and gathers the papers.

Annoyance washes over me at the sight of her, especially when my eyes land on her giant engagement ring she loves to flaunt.

She's the chick Decker hooked up with from Dallas. She's from The Hunter Group, a firm we recently merged with and now she's Decker's fiancée. She's practically the opposite of Quinn in every way imaginable.

Things have smoothed over a little since the merger, but she can still be an uppity bitch who thinks she runs things. Pushy is an understatement with her. The best is when she tries to boss me around.

I'm not Decker and I'll be damned if I let her lead me around by the balls.

"Such a good Samaritan, Tate. I'll put you in for employee of the month."

"I'll be sure your name goes on the plaque for the alternates, down by the ladies room." Tate puts the papers on Quinn's desk and smirks.

Goddamn it.

The *Top Gun* reference would be hilarious if it came from anyone but her.

I walk into my office, over to my desk to check my schedule for next week. I have a court date coming up for a suit against a local heart surgeon named James Flynn. One of his nurses filed a complaint with the court, saying he smacked her on the ass after a procedure and told her, "Well done."

I hate these types of cases. For one, it's he said, she said. Most of the time the accused is a guilty asshole, but I believe Flynn. He's been a surgeon for more than thirty years and everyone raves about the guy, including previous female employees. He doesn't have a single write up on his record. Not to mention he's like sixty and is a family man. The main thing, though, is I've talked to him and sized him up. You can tell he'd never do that shit.

It doesn't matter if I believe him, though. I need a judge to.

I pick up the phone to order Quinn flowers when Tate raps on my door.

I hang the phone up, surprised she actually knocked this time. "Come in."

I really want to ask her if she finished Decker's castration procedure and has his nuts in a jar, but I want her out of here as quickly as possible.

"How are preparations for the Flynn case coming along?"

My jaw clenches. "Just fine, *Tate*." I grate out her name.

"Doesn't look like it. You have time to run around being a bully and knocking shit on the floor but haven't watched the security video the hospital emailed over."

"I have an idea. Why don't you fetch me a coffee while I have myself a movie night with the video?" I smirk as all the color drains from her face.

That's right, Tate. Fuck off.

"Just watch the damn video. It's a lot like loading male male porn, all you have to do is click the little triangle in the middle. Shouldn't be anything you can't handle."

"That what does it for you and Decker?" I hold up both hands. "Not judging. I think it's great you two found some common ground in the bedroom."

She glares back at me. "Don't fuck this up."

"How about I give you a call the next time something more in your wheelhouse comes along? Like a ranch hand getting mauled by a heifer."

I belt out a moo as she storms out of the office.

Jesus Christ. She deserved that.

I don't take orders from her. She needs to get that shit through her thick head. I do need to review that video though, so I pull up my email. I'm sure there's nothing on it, but it would be really nice to catch a break.

My thoughts drift back to Quinn and how hot she looked with swollen lips and disheveled hair. Her pale skin and petite frame wrapped around me while she milked my cock for every last drop.

The video can wait a minute. I pick up the phone again and dial the florist. All women love flowers. I'd have my secretary handle this shit, but I don't need any gossip getting back to Quinn. She'd end our little fling in a heartbeat.

One thing is certain, though.

Quinn *will* be mine.

QUINN

I GET in line at the cafeteria to grab Decker's coffee and scroll through my task list for the morning. Hopefully, today will go smoothly and I can duck out an hour early to get a head start on my weekend. It doesn't happen often but on rare occasions Decker sends me home before five.

I move up a spot in line and browse the pastries in the display case. I didn't have time for breakfast. My power went out sometime during the night and I overslept. My company cell died, but thankfully my personal phone had a charge and my backup alarm woke me up.

My personal line buzzes inside my bag.

Great.

I can't ignore it. It could be my dad. He only calls for emergencies.

Digging through my wallet, lip gloss, and spare deodorant, I finally find it. My best friend Heather's face lights up on the screen.

"Hey. Everything okay?"

ALEX WOLF & SLOANE HOWELL

"Yeah. Just the usual. Getting ready to live that luxurious retail life."

"If you hate it so much why don't you quit?"

She works at some swanky store where one skirt costs more than my rent.

"Not everyone is a genius like you."

I can picture her sticking her tongue out at me as she says it. She can be such a brat, but I adore her. And I do enjoy the discount she gets me. I wouldn't have such nice work outfits without it. I make a decent salary but not enough for those kinds of clothes.

"Yeah, yeah. Hold on a second." I mute her and place my order. "Okay, I'm back." I balance the coffee holder with one hand and tuck the phone between my chin and shoulder while I stuff a muffin in my mouth.

She complains about her boss for most of the walk back to my floor. "Anyway, enough about that. What are you doing tonight?"

"Studying."

"C'mon, Quinn. Let's go out. It's Friday." Heather's been after me for weeks to go clubbing with her.

Between work and school, I don't have much time for a social life, which is why closet meetings with Deacon work for me.

"Carter Hughes will be there. He's been asking about you."

I roll my eyes. Carter Hughes is a prick who nails anything that spreads its legs for him. He's like a younger and even more immature version of Deacon. No thanks. One rich asshole is enough for me.

"Can't. I'll call you later. Just got back to my desk." I

end the call with Heather when I notice a large bouquet of flowers front and center. They come every Friday like clockwork. I keep throwing them in the trash, but Deacon won't take the hint.

I can't believe he keeps pulling this shit when someone might trace it back to him. I already know how the scenario would play out. He'd get a small reprimand from Decker, and I'd be shown the door.

Sometimes the hushed whispers and stares make me wonder if half the office doesn't already know. I'm almost positive Tate is on to us. I really need to put a complete stop to this madness before it gets out of control. I set the coffee holder on my desk and tuck my bag into the bottom drawer. I pluck the card from the flowers.

I will get a yes.

-D

"Secret admirer?" Decker's deep voice booms in my ear.

"Holy sh—" I clutch the card to my chest, my pulse throbbing in my ears. "Sorry. You scared me." I flip the card face down and hand Decker his coffee.

"How's today look?"

I take a moment to collect my thoughts.

Decker and Deacon are both tall and fit. Where Decker has icy blue eyes, Deacon's are gray and broody. Both men are attractive, but then again, all the Collins brothers are. They're about the same height, but Deacon is way bigger while Decker is lean. Deacon's damn biceps are like basketballs.

My gaze sweeps down the corridor toward Deacon's

office out of habit. A habit I need to break but can't seem to. Just like I can't seem to stop sleeping with him.

Decker clears his throat and snaps me out of my reverie.

"Right. You have a meeting with Beckley Brothers. Potential new client. They're a young construction company but growing fast. They need advice on some contracts. They built that new coffee place down the street that looks like a giant cup." I pray he doesn't pile a bunch of work on me for the weekend. I have a big test I need to study for.

"Everything's in order?"

I blink. "I'm sorry, what?"

"For the meeting? I need you focused, Quinn. Something going on with you?"

"No. I mean, right, of course. No worries. I'll have everything ready." I hope that was the answer he was looking for. We work together really well. A lot of people think he's an asshole, but he just likes things to run smoothly and hates repeating himself. Usually, I'm on the ball and anticipate his needs before he asks.

"Great."

I chuck the flowers in the trash once Decker heads toward his office.

Glancing around at my desk, I notice someone has been moving crap around again.

Damn it, Deacon.

This is one of the reasons I can't take his request for a date seriously. He's nothing but an immature office prankster with a big dick who behaves like a teenager.

Why does he get me so flustered?

I'm slipping. I'm off my game and it's all his fault.

I eye the box of chocolates sitting where my phone should be. It really would be a shame to waste them. They look super expensive.

"Who keeps sending the flowers you throw away?" Tate smirks when she walks up. I know she knows.

"This guy Carter. Won't take no for an answer." I roll my eyes, hoping my performance is believable. "Chocolate?" I thrust the box toward her.

"Maybe later."

I shrug. More for me.

I bite into a truffle and nearly have what I could only describe as a chocolategasm.

Man, these are good.

Now, I just need to figure out how to get myself out of this Deacon mess, after I've had a few more chocolates.

DEACON

I SNICKER at the flowers sitting in Quinn's trash can as I head to Decker's office.

I can't help but notice all the gold foil wrappers scattered through the petals.

Didn't throw those fucking chocolates away, did you Quinn?

I'll wear her down, slowly but surely.

She's away from her desk or I'd give her shit about it. I haven't seen her all day.

Dexter and I hit the golf course with some old oil tycoon Dexter's trying to land. Guy has a nine-digit net worth and is on his last legs. It took two hours longer than normal to play eighteen. I don't know how the guy hasn't pickled his goddamn liver. He drank a fifth of whiskey before the turn at hole nine. Even I can't stomach drinking that much that early. I like a good time as much as the next guy, but fuck.

Much respect to him.

When I checked in with my secretary earlier, she let

me know Tate dropped off a mountain of files on my desk. The hairs on the back of my neck stand up thinking about it. She does this shit just to piss me off, but I won't give her the satisfaction.

I walk into Decker's office.

His head pops up from whatever he was reading, like a damn meerkat. "You assholes need to start knocking."

"Get your woman on a leash, pussy. Your house is out of order and it's affecting me."

Decker stands up and his jaw flexes. "Watch your mouth." He bows up for a second, then relaxes. "You don't like Tate because she makes you work." Raking a hand through his hair, a smile slowly spreads across his face. "Actually, I have something even you can handle. Easy as shit and you're perfect for it. Do it and I'll tell Tate to ease up."

I rub my hands together. "Now we're talking, brother. Consider it done."

"I need you to speak at a college."

My jaw ticks and I stare at him.

He tries to hold back a laugh at my reaction, but he's damn near trembling.

Finally, I shake my head. "Fuck off. I'm not doing that. Have Dex do it." Decker knows I hate that kind of shit.

"Not up for debate. You already agreed and we might be The Hunter Group now, but I'm still the managing partner in Chicago." His face turns serious as he paces around his desk and leans back against it with his arms crossed. "If you want Tate off your ass, prove to me you can be an asset. Because, if we're being honest here, I'm getting sick of your shit. We're not just accountable to ourselves anymore. You bring in the least amount of clients, log the least amount of billable hours, you're out golfing all morning when Dexter could've gone by himself, and you reek of whiskey. So get your secretary or a paralegal to draft a presentation if you can't come up with one on your own."

I love how he talks shit about me smelling like whiskey when he has a whole goddamn bar in the corner. Regardless, I can see it written on his face that I'm not getting out of this. "Fine." I growl the word, a vein bulging in my neck. "When?"

"Monday night."

I sigh. "You shitting me? Night school? What the fuck, Decker? What if I have plans?"

He smiles. "A Pornhub marathon doesn't count as plans. The professor is a good friend and sends me clients and keeps an eye out for prospective employees. I want you to look for any possible students we might want to offer an internship."

"Night schoolers aren't real lawyers. Why would you hire someone from there?" I groan. I know exactly who goes to night school. People who don't have their lives together and people past their prime. Working adults who have way too much shit going on to be dedicated employees.

I know I'm being harsh, but my brain is searching for any reason it can possibly conjure for me to get out of this.

Decker straightens up in front of me. "Know what your problem is?"

I hold my hands up. "Please tell me, Dad."

"You're incapable of being an adult."

23

I scoff. "That's not true. I'm always mature."

"Really? How about the time you cut a hole in the bottom of a bag of Doritos, stuck your dick in it, then offered some to Donavan?"

I try to hold back my laugh. Fuck, that was a good one. "He had it coming." I can barely keep a straight face after that magnificent pun. It was a ten if I've ever heard one.

"It was during a staff meeting!"

"Well, he met with the staff, all right. And a lot of people would've been happy with his surprise."

Decker shakes his head and pinches the bridge of his nose. "What about the chart you made in Excel to rate the tits of our hottest clients?"

I point a finger at him, deadpanning a serious glare. "That was an exercise from a training seminar you sent me to. I was practicing pivot tables." I can't even look at him while I finish the last sentence.

"Jesus Christ. Enough. You're speaking at the college and I'll be following up to make sure you represented the firm in a professional manner."

"Fine. Can I fuck off now? Or is there anything else?"

"Go, please. This little chat is giving me a headache."

As I leave his office, Tate saunters by and gives me a side eye. I can practically hear them laughing at me from his office.

Oh, fuck both of you and your missionary sex.

She has him right by the pecker, leading him around and taking over the firm. Decker never had a problem with my performance until she showed up. Donavan told me all about her going to Decker to get one of his lawsuits dropped. Not everyone wants to work their ass off nonstop and never enjoy life like Decker and Tate. They live for their jobs. Some of us have a fucking life and actually enjoy cracking a joke and laughing once in a while.

Bitter old fucks, and they're not even old yet.

Besides, I fill a role and it's perfect for me. I'm the charismatic brother. The one who goes out and drinks with the good ol' boys. I warm them up and then Decker comes in and closes the deal at the end.

The only problem is he takes all the credit for landing them and acts like I don't do shit.

Fuck him.

I go out on the weekends and schmooze while he's at home being a dad in his giant house. I endure countless hangovers for this firm, thank you very much. And I never bitch about my job like Decker. He's turning into a woman. I bet Tate has a bigger dick than his.

I smile at my thoughts, loving the way I rationalize partying as an asset to the company. I am who I am. At least I don't pretend to be something I'm not.

QUINN

DROPPING my bag on the counter, I rifle through it for a tie and pull my hair up into a messy bun. I'm ready to kick my heels off and change out of these stuffy clothes. It's been a long week and I need to make dinner for Dad and settle in to study.

It's just the two of us.

"That you, Quinn?" my father calls from the living room of our two-bedroom apartment. The place has a weird floor plan. The hallway leads past a coat closet then a half bathroom and the kitchen. The living room is just beyond, then a full bath split between two bedrooms. We live on the bottom floor because Dad needs an electric wheelchair to get around. He suffered a stroke a few years ago. It left him with severe nerve damage down his right side and forced him into early retirement. Before that, he drove a bus for the city.

"No, it's Publisher's Clearing House. We won a million bucks." I giggle. It's an ongoing joke between the two of us.

He rolls toward the kitchen using his regular wheelchair, and I smile. He's having a good day if he can wheel himself around, and it's great for his arms to get a workout.

"Heather called. Said you told her you can't go out tonight." His eyes pierce through me.

"Don't start. I have a big exam next week."

"I'm going next door for dinner. Mrs. Waters is making enchiladas." He flashes his crooked grin. The stroke left him with a small droop on the right corner of his mouth.

"You know you'll regret it later when your heartburn hits. You aren't supposed to have that stuff."

"You go out with Heather and I'll lay off the hot sauce. You need to have a life once in a while."

I sit there and mull it over, glancing to the ceiling then back at him. "Fine, old man. I don't appreciate you using your health to hold me hostage."

"Who are you calling old? I'm fit as a fiddle."

"Yeah, yeah." I grab my bag and move around him, so I can call Heather and see what she's dragging me into this time.

"Dayumm. You look hot. If I was into women, I'd be all about this." Heather grins and waves a hand up and down at me.

She's wearing a red dress with see-through mesh that goes up both sides and down the front. She looks fantastic, but her outfit leaves little to the imagination. Her hair is swept up in a high ponytail and sways from side to side as she walks.

"Shut up." I fidget with my hair, smoothing it over my shoulders. "It's not too much?" I don't normally wear clothes this revealing, but Heather snagged the emerald-green dress for me from her store. They were going to toss it because a thread on the hem was frayed and needed replaced.

The front and back has a deep V that runs down to my navel and my rear. I couldn't even wear a bra with it. Paired with my auburn hair, I feel a bit like Poison Ivy.

It's packed wall to wall when we walk inside PRYSM Nightclub. Strobe lights flash off the wall and the thumping bass vibrates in my chest. Being packed in the place makes me a bit claustrophobic but nothing some booze can't handle.

"Let's get a drink." Heather has to yell in my ear.

I nod.

She gestures toward the bar and we navigate our way through the crowd of catcalls and wandering hands. I'm going to regret this tomorrow morning, but I'm already here, so I push the thought from my mind. I've missed hanging out with her and I'm always responsible. I can afford to let my hair down for once and have fun.

Heather goes on dates all the time. She eats up the single life since she ended things with her last boyfriend.

I order a whiskey sour. Heather gets a dirty martini. Drinks in hand, we look for a table, but it doesn't appear promising.

Just have a good time. It'll be fine.

I take a healthy swig from the rocks glass and sway my

hips to the music. I should've ordered two drinks, judging by the length of the line at the bar, but I need to pace myself.

We aren't in the club for more than five minutes when my face flushes and a familiar tingling fans out to my extremities.

It's not the alcohol.

I glance up to the second floor that overlooks the main dance area.

It's him.

Deacon.

He's chatting up some busty brunette that's fawning all over him. He smiles right at her.

It's a smile some part of my brain hoped was reserved for just me.

I know better but seeing it still stings. He's in his element, doing what he does best—charming women.

I'm an idiot.

I shouldn't feel foolish, but that's exactly how I feel right now. I know he sees other people. I tell myself constantly I hope he finds someone to take his attention away from me. He'll never settle down with one woman.

The music cuts off just as Heather shouts my name. "Quinn!"

His eyes flash in the direction of her voice, but I dart out of his line of sight praying he didn't see me.

"You okay?" Heather eyes me, giving me a once over.

"Good. Just a little overwhelmed." I suck down my drink. "Maybe this wasn't the best idea. I'm not really feeling it."

"Okay." She frowns and knocks her martini back. "Let's get out of here."

I nod.

We place our empty glasses on a nearby table and move toward the exit. The lights dim, and they're replaced with neons strobing across the ceiling.

I turn my head and catch a glimpse at the spot where Deacon stood earlier but he's gone.

"What do we have here?" A deep voice rumbles in my ear, and a hard body presses into me from behind.

For a brief moment, I smile. I shouldn't, but I do. It has to be Deacon.

I turn around and the smile fades immediately. Carter Hughes wraps a hand around my waist like he just won the lottery.

In all honesty, if I didn't know him, I'd probably find him attractive. Unfortunately, I do know him. We fooled around for a bit in high school. Actually, he strung me along under the guise of dating, while he slept with several of my so-called friends.

The joys of high school.

I shoot him a look that says *let go of me now* and move away, but he tightens his grip and pulls me closer. I smell whiskey on his breath, and he slurs his words like he's hammered. Heather is a few feet away talking to one of his friends, Stewart. I already know this is a set up, but I can't be too mad at her. I never really told her about my history with Carter out of embarrassment. I never really tell her about my sex life at all. I thought I'd hinted I wasn't interested in him, but apparently, I didn't communicate it effectively.

I try to squirm my way out of Carter's grip, but Stewart guides Heather toward the bar. She must've seen my initial smile and thought I was okay with Carter. That has to be it.

Great.

Now I'm on my own with this asshole. She better not leave me here alone and go home with Stewart.

"Fuck, you got hot." Carter exhales in my ear, and I shudder.

"Thanks." I sigh and twist out of his grip. "I'm going to the bathroom."

"Want some company in there?"

"That's the exact opposite of what I want."

"Well, don't keep me waiting." He leans in to kiss me, and I duck out of the way.

He damn near stumbles into someone else, and I make my escape.

DEACON

GOD, this place sucks a dick.

This club isn't my style, but I promised to show a client's son a night on the town and he wanted to come here. Wrenley Cooper is new to Chicago. He grew up on the West Coast with his alcoholic former child star mother. His father, Justice Cooper owns one of the biggest recording companies on the planet and he's grooming Wrenley to join the family business.

Good luck with that, Mr. Cooper.

He's fresh out of college and a fucking nerd. He's the exact opposite of his parents, and I can't help but feel bad for the kid, and good for him in a certain way. His dad's an asshole of the highest order, but he's definitely good for padding my billable hours and nets me a nice little bonus each quarter.

The kid looks uncomfortable as fuck in this place, like he'd rather be off playing Call of Duty. Why the hell did he ask to come here? Maybe he's just awkward.

I think Justice hopes I'll get the kid laid. You know the

dynamic I'm talking about. Father and son who are night and day different. Kid wants to play computer games. Dad wants him to be a man and live up to the family name, rush a fraternity, run naked through the quad up to the gymnasium type shit.

It's kind of sad, and I can relate to the kid. I know what it's like to live in the shadow of family and not meet expectations.

I chat up this ditzy-ass chick for him. Her tits are about the only thing she has going for her, because the brain cells are lacking. Maybe she's dumb enough to give the kid a blow jay and get his father off both our backs.

Just about the time she starts to regale me with her supreme intelligence, I hear someone shout the name Quinn. My head jerks and I scan the club looking for the auburn-haired woman who loves to tease my cock every chance she gets. It's wishful thinking. There's no way in fuck she'll be caught dead in this place. It's so not—her. Hell, I don't have a clue what she does outside of working at the firm. That's one of the reasons she needs to stop being so goddamn stubborn and go on a date with me. I want to know what she likes to do. I want to get to know her better.

"You're like hot." The chick giggles.

I manage not to roll my eyes. It's all about ol' Wren's dick tonight. I can't be an asshole to her until the mission is accomplished.

"Speaking of hot, you should meet my friend. He could use some company. His girlfriend dumped his ass." I sigh and nod. "Yeah, she really did a number on the poor guy. Dumb decision. He's rich as fuck."

Her nose scrunches up. "What's wrong? Why'd she dump him?"

I lean in close and whisper in her ear. "This is just between us. You can never tell him I told you this."

Her eyes widen. This shit is too fucking easy.

"Okay, I promise."

"She couldn't handle his dick."

She leans back a little, like she's feigning offense.

I shrug and look off at the crowd, scanning for Quinn but putting on a show at the same time. "It's true."

Her eyes dart over to Wrenley.

Fuck, he's standing there looking all pathetic.

"You sure?"

I shrug. "It's always the shy ones. You know this. They don't need to brag."

Her lips curl into a grin. "He *is* kind of cute, but I was hoping you'd take me home." She bumps me with her hip and splays her fingers across my chest over my shirt.

Fucking hell. This chick is thirsty as shit. "Tell you what. You show Wrenley a good time and *maybe* if he reports good things, I'll consider it."

"What?" Her brow wrinkles in disgust.

I can't help but smile on the inside. I'm like a great stand-up comedian. Sometimes you have to lead the audience into dark territory, just to bring them back out of it to make the laughs that much sweeter. "You heard me." I smirk.

"Ugh. You're an…"

"Asshole." I finish the sentence for her. "I know, and you love that about me. Just have a fucking drink with the guy. It's his birthday."

Her brows shoot up. "I thought you said his girlfriend broke up with him?"

Maybe she has a few brain cells after all, but not many. I shake my head. "Terrible isn't it? No guy should get dumped on his birthday because he's packing a huge dick." I shrug and signal for another drink.

I watch the gears turning in this chick's head as she looks over Wrenley.

Fuck, he's a train wreck, but he reeks of money. I already know this chick can smell it on him. She has dollar signs in her eyes.

"I suppose one drink won't kill me." She squares her shoulders, pushes her tits out, and walks over to him. She hooks her arms around his neck and plants a kiss right on his lips, smearing hooker-red lipstick all over his mouth.

It's too fucking easy sometimes.

A hand shoots out behind the woman's back and flashes me a thumbs up.

My work here is done.

Now, what the fuck am I going to do while this kid gets his cock shined?

I scan the dance floor, looking for anyone I might know so I won't be bored out of my mind.

That's when I see her.

My heart tries to pound its way out of my chest.

Quinn walks toward the door in a sinful green dress that hugs her body in all the right places. My cock twitches and starts to rise at the sight. God, I've never seen her look so fucking hot. She's like supermodel fucking beautiful.

Just as my mind races to think of how and where I could fuck her in the club and take our sexcapades to a whole new level, some asshole wraps his arm around her waist and yanks her close to him.

My blood heats to a million degrees and I wouldn't be surprised if steam shoots out of my ears. That son of a bitch is touching what's mine.

I take off for the stairs.

It doesn't take long for me to practically sprint toward her. I knock a few people out of the way and spill their drinks, but I don't give a shit. I move toward the exit, attempting to track her every move but I keep losing sight of her. Just as I start to intervene, she scoffs at the guy and takes off toward the bathroom.

That's my girl.

He stares at her as she navigates through the crowd toward the ladies' room.

"You can fuck right off, sir." I mutter the words under my breath and angle to cut her off before she gets to her destination.

Just as she's about to enter the bathroom, I grip her forearm and pull her over to the corner.

Her eyes dart around for a second, and she looks like she might scream. Then her stare lands on my face. Her tempting lips form an amused grin and she shakes her head. "What are you doing here?"

I rake my eyes up and down her dress and try not to blow a load in my pants just at the sight of her. "Me?" I raise my brows at her.

Our gazes lock and I lick my lips wanting nothing more than to shove her against the wall and have my way with her.

"You on a date?"

"What if I am?"

"I'd want to know his Jedi secrets since you keep turning me down."

She shakes her head in a playful way. "Maybe he's just nice and acts like a grown up."

I shrug and flash her a smile. "Unfortunate for him."

"Oh really?" She grins, clearly amused with our conversation. "Because he landed a date with me and you couldn't?"

"Absolutely."

"And why would that be unfortunate for him? I'm dying to know."

"Because he did all that work. Acted like such an adult. Probably took you to dinner, picked you up, drove you here." I lean in close, so she can feel my warm breath in her ear. "And I'll be the one who takes you home and fucks you."

"Now, that's funny." Quinn tries to play it off like we're joking, but I notice every single one of her reactions when I tell her that. Her breath catches in her throat, her words stammer ever so slightly. The pulse on the side of her neck speeds up, right in the place I want to run my tongue.

I lean back and smile. "It is what it is. Let's get out of here."

"No way. We shouldn't even be seen together."

"Who's going to see? I can have a hotel suite in five minutes."

Quinn laughs. "I'm not going to a hotel with you."

"Oh, but you'll fuck me in a broom closet at work?"

Her eyes narrow. "You're an asshole. Why don't you

go find that skank you were flirting with? I'm sure she'd love to go to your hotel suite." She makes air quotes when she says "hotel suite."

"Oh, so you saw me and weren't even going to come say hi? Real mature, Quinn." God, I love it when she gets all worked up. "If I didn't know better, I'd think you're jealous."

"Not even."

"Quinn?" The asshole who had his arm around her walks up. Must've gotten tired of waiting. "Is this guy bothering you?"

I flash him a stare reserved for my worst enemies. "I'm her boss, fuck head. Get lost."

He shrinks back, holding his palms up.

Pussy.

"Real nice." Quinn smacks my arm with her palm.

"I never claimed to be nice." I grin. "Let me at least buy you a drink. I've been trying to get you alone outside the office for months. Don't shit on my one opportunity."

Quinn's eyes dart around the club, then she points a finger at me. "One drink. That's it. No funny business."

Business is the farthest thing from my mind. I wrap an arm around her waist and guide her toward the back. I shoot the asshole a look that says *stay the fuck away from her* as we move to the bar.

When we reach our destination, I move her in front of me. The place is so packed it pushes my cock right up against her ass.

Sliding my arm around her waist, I bury my nose in her hair and inhale. The amount of restraint it takes to not rip her dress off and fuck her on the bar is unworldly.

39

"Vodka cranberry." I order for her.

"What if I don't like cranberries?"

"You like them." I cage her in at the bar grazing the shell of her ear with my teeth. I love how she pretends I've never seen her drinking cranberry juice at the office. Like I don't pay attention to every goddamn detail when it comes to her.

"This is trouble."

"No one from the office is here. You worry too much." I slide my hand down the front of her dress under the privacy of the bar. I make sure to graze just along her clit, but not quite touching it. It's not my fault the deep v cut in the front of her dress gives me easy access to her pussy.

"Deacon." She lets out a gasp.

I remove my hand quickly when the bartender walks over with her drink.

Quinn drinks faster than she needs to. "Well, we had a drink."

"You made me a happy man." I slide my hand back down the front of her dress and venture a little farther this time.

Her lips part ever so slightly when I circle her clit with the tip of my finger.

I lean in close to her ear. "You can pretend you want to get out of here all you want, Quinn. Your pussy tells a different story."

"God, I really hate you sometimes." She says the words, but her hips grind against my hand at the same time.

Her eyes flash up to mine, but then she looks past me.

Something or someone catches her attention. She jerks away from me and hauls ass through the crowd.

What the fuck?

Quinn stomps off toward the exit.

Like a dog in heat, I give chase. Finally, I grip her by the forearm and spin her around to face me. "Where you going?"

"Home. Alone." She looks away and types furiously on her phone.

"I'll give you a ride."

"No!" She rushes out of the building.

I run after her, but a cab pulls up and Quinn slides inside. She slams the door in my face before I can get to her, and the car speeds off.

What the hell?

QUINN

I sneak off to my favorite coffee shop to nurse my hangover and study for my upcoming test. Dad has a physical therapy appointment and it gives me a few hours to myself. I knew going out last night was a terrible idea.

Any time Deacon's near it's nothing but trouble. The second I let my guard down, I saw two new girls from the Dallas office watching us. At least I think they saw me. I wasn't about to stick around to find out.

No way.

"Refill?"

I smile at the server. "Please and can I get a chocolate scone?"

"Definitely." She takes my cup, and my phone buzzes. I check it, in case it's Dad and something has happened.

It's Heather.

Heather: Holy shit! I went home with Stewart last night after I got your text and let's just say dude has a helicopter for a tongue. You make it home okay? Carter said your boss threatened him. I need details.

I can't help but shake my head as I read over her message. She's so open about her sex life and I'm so guarded with mine. I never told her about Deacon. Part of me feels like a bad friend, but it's my personal information. I don't share it with anyone.

Speaking of Deacon. He won't stop blowing up my phone asking for an explanation. It *was* a little sweet, him constantly texting to see if I made it home okay.

I ignore everyone and try to focus on my notes. I'm ahead of schedule, at least. There's a guest speaker Monday so we won't cover anything new. I decide to fire off a response to Heather as the server sets down my coffee and scone.

Quinn: He thought Carter was bugging me. Which he was. I'm in the middle of cramming for my test. Dinner tonight?

Heather: Depends on if Stewart calls. I think I might like him.

Quinn: Okay, keep me posted. Talk later.

I roll my eyes. She could do so much better than him, but I want to be supportive. Who am I to judge anyway? It's not like I'm killing it in the decision-making department.

My phone pings again. This time it's another message from Deacon.

Deacon: It's Saturday. You should be in my bed, naked.

I try like hell to fight the smile spreading across my face when I read his message. My body screams at me, but I can't risk it. I do find immense pleasure in messing with him, though. I stare at my phone. Should I respond? I fire off a reply before I chicken out.

Quinn: Maybe I'm already naked. Ever consider that?
Deacon: Pictures or it didn't happen.

My cheeks bloom with pink when I read his message.

Know what? To hell with it.

Tucking my laptop in my bag, I gather my things and duck into the bathroom. I can't believe I'm even considering doing this…sending Deacon a picture.

As long as I don't show my face there's no proof it's me and we're texting on my personal phone. I lock the door behind me, place my bag on the sink, and unbutton my shirt, exposing my bra. I've never done anything like this and it's far more awkward than I imagined. Zooming in on my chest, I snap a shot of my cleavage and hit send.

My work cell buzzes in my bag and panic floods my bloodstream. What if it's Deacon messaging me from a company phone? I'm scared to check the message, but I can't be a chicken shit. It's stupid anyway. Deacon wouldn't be that dumb.

I swipe my thumb across the screen and there's an email from Decker. He needs me to come in today and deliver some contracts to the Beckley brothers.

Shit.

It's rare for him to ask for anything on a Saturday, especially after the merger. He never works weekends anymore but I'm already out and it's my job.

I fire off a reply to Decker telling him I'm on it, then call my dad.

"Hey, sweetie."

"I'm going to be a little late. Need to run to the office."

"I'm beat from my appointment. Gonna take a nap."

"You sure you're okay?"

"Stop worrying so much, Mom!" He hangs up on me.

I can't help but smile.

I shouldn't feel guilty for leaving him on his own because it's work related, but I do.

I ARRIVE at the firm twenty minutes later and one of the weekend security guys holds the door for me.

"Mr. Collins is in his office."

I frown but maybe he means one of the other brothers. If Decker was here, he could deliver the contracts himself.

"Thanks. I won't be long."

"Take your time."

I step into the elevator. The doors close and I press the button for my floor. When I get off the elevator, I drop my stuff on my desk. Decker's office is locked, and the lights are shut off. Maybe the security guy was mistaken. I trek back to my desk and fetch my key to Decker's office from the top drawer. Before I stick the key in the lock, I sense a presence and a hand clamps over my mouth.

"Knew I'd get you here." Deacon's voice grates in my ear and the scent of his cologne washes over me. "Such a dedicated little employee."

I spin around ready to smack the piss out of him. "You sent that email, didn't you? Is there even a contract?"

"Yeah, but it's not ready yet." Deacon grins. "I wanted to see you."

"Well you saw me." I stomp toward my desk to grab my stuff and head home.

"Come on, Quinn. Fuck." He takes a step toward me. "You have to appreciate the effort I put in to get you alone." He flashes me his pearly whites with a shit-eating grin.

"You're out of control," I hiss at him.

He shrugs as if my job isn't at stake with his antics. "I asked you out to dinner, but you said no."

I wrap my arms around my waist and look away. "We both know I'll end up hurt. Please, stop doing this to me."

"You don't know that." He steps into my personal space and drags a finger down my throat. He nods down the hall. "Come to my office. Give me five minutes."

I shake my head.

"I won't do anything you don't want me to."

"Deacon, I…"

"Stop thinking so much. It's exhausting."

He grips my hand and pulls me with him. Like an idiot, I follow, knowing I'm making a huge mistake. At the same time, butterflies swarm my stomach, the way they do every time he so much as looks in my direction.

What is wrong with me?

I shouldn't entertain the idea of dating Deacon. We both know what will happen. After the newness and excitement wears off, he'll cheat on me or I'll accidentally end up pregnant.

He's not mature enough to handle a real relationship or responsibility. It's why he always wears a condom, even though I'm on the pill. I'm not taking any chances.

We get to his office and he locks the door behind him

but doesn't bother to close the blinds. Not that I'm going to do anything with him. He can have his five minutes then I'm out of here. In fact, as soon as he's done with his little speech, I'm ending this whole thing. It's not worth it. Never was.

He wheels around on me once we're inside and his face is tense. "Why do you keep fighting this?" He wags a finger between us.

"Just stop, okay? This isn't happening in here."

He grins and takes a step toward me. "We both know that's a lie."

"Deacon, I..." I take a step away from him, and my back slams into the door as he stalks toward me like a hungry lion.

I try to think of all the things I want to say to him, to end this little charade, but my brain is a jumbled mess when he stares at me like that.

I start to say something, and he puts his index finger to my lips.

"Shh. We're not here to talk." A devilish smirk crosses his face, and I lose all train of thought when his hand cups my jaw and his lips crash down on mine. He keeps talking as he kisses me. "What do I have to do to show you this is real? Huh, Quinn?" His rough hands grip my ass and yank me into him. His teeth nip at my neck. "I want you. All of you. I want to know what you're thinking." His tongue slides up the side of my neck to beneath my ear. "What you do outside of work."

"Deacon, please..."

"I want you all the time. Not just in a fucking closet."

"We can't." My words come out on a shallow gasp as his hand massages my breast.

He's so hungry and possessive, and sweet and sincere at the same time. How the hell does he do this to me? I allow myself to believe the lie a little longer. That maybe something more is possible. That we could be more than just a fling.

I already know as soon as I step away and analyze the situation, I'll go right back to not trusting him. To wanting to end whatever this is between us, but it's impossible right now with him brooding in front of me.

"We can. Just say yes, goddamn it."

It's impossible to deny the attraction, the way my heart races in my chest. "Why can't I stay away from you?" I grip his shirt in my hands and without thinking, yank it up from his pants. Next, I go to work on the buttons, exposing the chiseled lines of his abs. He definitely works out. He's not as lean as the other Collins brothers. Deacon is thick and strong, but his muscles are still well defined.

"It's cute when you try to take charge." He smiles against my lips, running his finger along the curve of my jaw and down my neck. His fingertip burns a trail along my exposed skin. "I need you naked."

My body reacts to his command before I can even question it. I pull my top over my head and kick off my shoes. Deacon grabs the drawstring of my sweatpants and jerks me forward. He's never seen me dressed this casual before. I'm always in skirts and jackets. I silently pray I'm wearing decent underwear. After my shower this morning I think I just threw on whatever was clean, and I can't remember what it was. He smirks at me when he pushes

49

my pants to the floor. I look down and realize I'm not wearing any.

His eyebrows lift. "You came prepared." Reaching around my back with one hand and two fingers, Deacon skillfully removes my bra and flings it across the room. "Fuck, you're hot. I've never seen you completely naked before." He steps back and looks me up and down like he's appraising me.

I back up to the wall. "What about security?"

"He won't come up here. Trust me."

Part of me hates Deacon for planning this, and that his plan is clearly working.

I'm already naked and definitely going through with it, so I might as well enjoy myself. I strut past him and bend over his desk. When I know he's looking, I wiggle my ass at him. "Well, what are you waiting for?"

In no time he's behind me, his hard cock pressed up against my ass.

The smug bastard loves taunting me. His teeth sink into my shoulder, and I feel him free his cock. He slides the crown across my clit, and I can already feel the pending orgasm throbbing between my legs. Rocking my hips, I grind against him, craving more.

"You have no idea how bad I want you bare. Fuck."

I glance back and smile when he pulls the condom from his pocket. Some things are non-negotiable, no matter how ridiculous my brain decides to act.

Part of me smiles on the inside that even though Deacon is the most irresponsible human being I've ever met, he doesn't fight me on the issue. It's like he can sense where to press his luck and where not to. Despite his immaturity, he's very intelligent when he needs to be.

Once he's ready, he gives my ass a playful smack.

A light coo escapes my lips.

"I want to take my time with you, but I don't know if I'll be able to." He eases into me from behind. "So. Fucking. Tight."

The suddenness of him filling me from within is almost too much to bear. Why does he have to be so damn good at this? Why do his words do this to me?

"You don't know how long I've wanted you here, just like this." One of his hands grips my hip, the other lands on my shoulder. "Bent over my desk."

His hips speed up as his fingers dig in and yank me back to meet each thrust.

"I'm so close."

Without warning, he lifts one of my legs up onto the desk, and just like that he's even deeper.

So deep.

He's hitting places I didn't know existed and his hand slips around my waist. His finger circles my clit and I'm two seconds away from being in the clouds.

Deacon leans over and his mouth is next to my ear as his thighs crash into me. "I know every button to push. Nobody knows what you like more than I do, Quinn."

"God, Deacon, I'm so…"

"Come for me. I want to feel you."

And just like that, his words send me over the edge and I'm free falling. My thighs quiver and my body shakes. The orgasm rushes through me like a wild, uncontrolled river. Fuzzy stars appear in front of my eyes and I don't know how I'm still able to stand.

Deacon slides out of me, whips me around, and before I know what's happened my ass is on his desk and he's spreading my legs. He drops to his knees and his mouth is on me, his eyes staring up into mine as he suckles my clit between his teeth.

I fall back on my elbows, barely able to support myself.

Deacon pushes a finger slowly inside me while he watches every reaction on my face. I can barely focus on his two gray eyes as he works a second finger in.

Another orgasm builds in my center and it won't be long before I'm coming all over his mouth.

"There's nothing better than watching you come for me."

I grip the edge of the desk, holding on for life. The second I'm about to release, he pulls away and stands back up.

He bends over and presses his forehead to mine, both of us panting, unable to form words, just staring into each other's eyes.

"Nothing better." He slides his cock back into me as he says the words, and a light groan comes from deep in his throat.

It's so sweet and intimate, almost like we're making love instead of just having sex. Deacon's hand cradles the back of my neck, and he pushes in and out, long deep strokes. Staring right at me, he licks the pad of his thumb, then reaches between us and rubs my clit.

Our eyes remain locked as he slowly increases the tempo, and before long we're fucking hard and fast.

His jaw constricts, and every muscle in his body tenses, just as my entire body reciprocates.

His thumb is relentless, right where I need it, and his hips crash into me until the wet slapping sounds of our skin echo through his office. My head falls back and I can't contain it anymore.

Deacon's mouth instinctively moves to my neck and he kisses me in that magic spot halfway between my collar bone and ear.

"Fuck, Quinn…"

My fingers grip the desk just as Deacon grunts. He slams into me as deep as he can go and we both erupt at the same time.

I clench around him so hard I wonder if it's painful for him. If it is, he doesn't show it. His entire body goes rigid as he fills the condom.

After a few long seconds, our foreheads meet again. We both pant, our lips inches apart, eyes locked.

I wait for some smart-ass remark that usually follows, but it doesn't come. He looks out of it, almost like he's in a dream-like state.

Deacon collapses into my neck, his lips on my skin, and I swear he whispers, "You're everything to me."

What the hell was that?

After a few seconds, he straightens up and his breathing returns to normal. "Fuck, I was good, wasn't I?"

That's more like him.

DEACON

"Fuck."

I run my fingers through my hair and rifle through my office for the stupid presentation I had Mary Magdalene, one of the paralegals, draft for me. I don't know her real last name, so that's the name we all gave her. She's always reading a bible at lunch and doesn't booze at all, so I figured she takes pride in her work.

There's a PowerPoint on my laptop, but she printed out the slides and I want to study them at least once. I have the speaking engagement at the college tonight.

Fucking Decker.

I'll get his ass back for this. He should know better. No sleight against me goes unpunished. I really need to read over those slides, so I sound like I know what the fuck I'm talking about. Can't be up there like it's amateur hour.

I should've faked being sick or canceled, but Decker would have my ass. I don't even want to imagine the pleasure it would give Tate.

Oh, no. They expect me to fuck up. They hope I will, to prove them right.

I'm going to crush this presentation and toss it back in their faces. I know exactly how they all see me. The immature brother who doesn't take anything seriously. The class clown. I know my role and I play it well. It is what it is.

One thing bothers me, though—Quinn.

I have this urge to do better, so she'll take me more seriously. It goes against everything I know, who I am.

Get out of your head, bro.

I find the print-out and start toward the elevator. I still have to finish up this contract for the Beckley brothers. I'll have to do it at home. Tate wanted it on her desk this morning, but I had to meet with the doctor over his sexual harassment case. I didn't find shit on the video, so it sucked giving him that news. Still, I know he didn't do anything, and I'll be damned if he pays his accuser a dime.

I'm sure I'll hear all about the contract being late. She knows I have a lot of stuff going on, but she won't give a shit.

"Ready for your lecture, professor?" Donavan laughs.

Asshole.

Decker ran his mouth and told everyone apparently.

"You're not going in that suit, are you?"

I stare back at him like *what the fuck are you talking about?*

"Shouldn't it be tweed with some elbow patches, Robert Langdon?"

"How's this for an ancient symbol?" I hold up my

middle finger. "What's wrong? Bitter about your soon-to-be sister-in-law putting her dick in your lawsuit?"

Donavan's face steams up and he marches off. Pussy. Don't make jokes if you can't take the heat. I thought it was fantastic. Burned him and Tate at the same time, while calling Decker's masculinity into question. That's the trifecta—a fucking work of art. Layers upon layers of comedy, bitch.

Just when I think I have a second to relax, Dex walks up. "Don't fret, professor. I know what you're worried about."

"What's that?"

He adjusts my tie and tries to maintain a serious face. "Worried you're not qualified to instruct an intro to law class. It's a natural cause for concern, given your background in academia."

"This coming from the guy who made a C in intro to law. You should be mopping floors here."

Dex laughs. At least he doesn't take shit seriously like Donavan. God, he's been a real asshole lately.

"Then I could solve your cases at night on a blackboard, *Good Will Hunting* style."

"Yeah, yeah, I tossed that softball right down the fucking middle. Anyway, enjoy your night beating off to iPad porn while I'm balls-deep in college pussy."

"Nah, something tells me you won't even be looking at any of the chicks in there." An amused smile forms on his face.

What does he know?

I shrug it off. "Probably not. I'm sure it'll be a bunch of old bastards in their forties."

"Dude, you're in your thirties."

I shake my head. "Who the fuck goes to night school to be a lawyer?"

Dexter grins. "Anyway, that's not the reason."

Shit.

"Oh yeah? Enlighten me."

His eyebrows rise. "You're really gonna make me say it?"

I know people always talk about how twins have a connection, like they can sense things. You'd think they'd be full of shit, but they're not. I can take one look at him and see he knows I'm falling for someone. I don't know how, but he does.

I sigh. "No. Don't say it."

"All right, then. Go crush it. Picture your audience naked. I hear it helps."

"I'll picture you naked, big boy." I give a playful slap at his crotch and he leaps backward.

"Over the line."

"Nothing is off limits."

Dexter laughs and walks off. I head to the elevator. As the doors shut, I hear Decker running his mouth off in the background and more raucous laughter.

Assholes.

AT MY APARTMENT, I heat some leftovers from last night and pull the Beckley brothers' contract up on my laptop. They won a bid for a restoration project on a hotel. All the details seem to be in order except for the payment schedule we discussed. I read over the notes of the agreement and shovel a forkful of pasta into my mouth. Sauce splatters on my white Brioni shirt.

Fuck.

I look at the clock and realize I'll be late if I don't get moving. I punch in the number, mark it final, and send it to Quinn so she can get it delivered.

It's supposed to go through review, but I only changed one number and I'm already late getting it out the door.

I breathe a sigh of relief. Tecker (my new name for Tate and Decker) can get off my nuts now.

Typing Quinn's name on the screen brings up familiar feelings all over again. I haven't talked to her since I bent her over my desk.

You don't have time to think about her right now.

The voice in my head is correct for once. I change my shirt and give myself a once over in the mirror.

"Well, damn. You clean up nice, sir, if I do say so myself."

QUINN

I TAKE my usual seat at the front of the class, eager to find out who the guest speaker is.

I've always been a great student, ever since elementary school. If things had gone according to plan, I'd already be on a partner track and not a glorified secretary.

It is what it is. Dad had the stroke. I can't change the past, and I'll never complain about sacrificing my plans to care for him.

It eats at him enough as it is.

Taking care of family is what you do. He raised me by himself, and I would never abandon him for my own selfish reasons. If I have to work twice as hard as everyone else to achieve the same outcome, that's what I'll do.

I never thought I'd be the one taking care of him, though. It's difficult sometimes. Not the work, per se, but seeing him in this condition. He was so damn strong and independent when I was younger.

He'd never brushed a little girl's hair or played with

Barbie Dolls, and he never complained once. He took care of me and pushed me to do my best. He still does.

The stroke turned our lives upside down. Taking care of him is hard work. His medications. His diet. Exercise. It's a lot for me to take on while working a full-time job and going to school, but I love the fact he knows I'm in his corner, that he doesn't have to face these challenges alone. Not a lot of people have that type of support system. And I get to hang out with him more than I would've under other circumstances. It helps get through the days to focus on the positive.

"Who do you think it's going to be?" Jillian slides into the seat next to mine.

We're basically the two eggheads who ask a ton of questions. Sometimes it elicits groans from the other students when our discussions push us past the end of class. I don't really care, though. I'm here to learn and get my money's worth.

"Don't have a clue." I smile at her.

She's a recently divorced single mom trying to provide a better future for her kids.

"I hope they're not as boring as the last one."

"Yeah, it's tough to make the tax code interesting, so I can't knock the guy too much."

Professor Billings enters the room and the place grows quiet.

"Good evening, everyone. We have a guest tonight. He's a man who could be your boss someday. Please give a warm welcome to Deacon Collins from The Hunter Group."

What in the fucking fuck? This can't be happening to me.

My mouth goes dry and my stomach twists in a knot. The color drains from my face when I look up and see Deacon.

He spots me on the front row and his eyes widen, then his lips curl into a grin and he winks.

I scowl back.

"Wow. I know where I want to work. Wonder if all the men at their firm are that hot?" Jillian mock fans herself.

If she only knew.

I bite my tongue to keep from saying something I'll regret. Like telling her he's off limits and mine. Or conversely, what a conceited asshole he is, or maybe how well he can use his hips and his tongue.

This can't be happening right now. My chest tightens and my stomach clenches at the thought of him bending me over his desk and making me come repeatedly.

Deacon gets his laptop and PowerPoint all set up. I know for a fact there's no way he put it all together. It looks like Mary's work. Of course, he didn't do the work himself, but he'll pull it all off because he's so damn charming and charismatic.

This is so damn embarrassing. I don't tell anyone in class where I work because my private life is just that... private. Also, I don't tell people from work I'm going to school at night. I don't want them to know that me, the assistant, wants to be a lawyer. A lot of lawyers at The Hunter Group are stuck up and don't think a secretary would be capable of doing their job. I've seen how some of them look down their noses at me.

Deacon starts up his lecture on tort law and how it's applicable in the real world. It's actually very helpful and I could learn a lot from it, but it's impossible to focus. All I keep thinking about is how I'm going to explain this to him later. There's no way he'll let it go.

"Seriously, though. How hot is this guy?" Jillian nudges me with her elbow when he unbuttons his sleeves and rolls them up his muscular forearms. "I wonder if I can get his number and get some help on Wednesday's exam."

Unable to control myself, I shoot her a dirty look when she raises her hand at the end of the lecture to ask questions, and I realize I'm being ridiculous.

I need to get the hell out of here before he talks to me.

I grab my stuff as quickly as I can and head for the door. I'm not sticking around to watch Jillian fawn all over him or hear one of his smart-ass remarks while he flirts with my classmate.

Jealousy courses through me as I rush from the building. I shouldn't feel this way, but this was my space. It was mine, and Deacon came barging through it like a wrecking ball. The thought of him asking Jillian out for drinks makes my blood run hot. I shouldn't care, but deep down I know one thing...

I do care.

A lot.

DEACON

IF QUINN CAN'T SEE the universe pushing us together, she needs her damn eyes examined. When I walked into the classroom and saw the open-toed heels she wore to work today, I couldn't contain the happiness that spread through my chest.

She rushes out of the classroom.

I interrupt some chick mid-sentence to chase after her. I had no idea Quinn wanted to be a lawyer. It makes sense. She'd be a damn good attorney.

I haul ass through the parking lot and catch her arm just as she's about to slide into the driver's side of her car.

"Where you running off to so fast? Going to get me an apple?" I grin. "In case you're wondering, yes, you *can* be the teacher's pet."

Her lips mash into a thin line and her body tenses. Shit. She looks pissed. Maybe it wasn't best to lead with a joke. I'm always fucking things up with her.

We both know she feels this spark between us. Why

she continually fights it I'll never know. It would be a hell of a lot easier if she'd just give in to the attraction.

Fuck, it would make me a happy man. The happiest.

She pulls out her keys, unable to say anything, and slides into the driver's seat. Her face is fiery red.

I reach inside and stop her from putting them in the ignition. "Look, I'm sorry. I didn't mean to joke. Let me take you to dinner."

"I'm not hungry." Her words are short and laced with venom.

"Coffee then?" I raise my eyebrows to try and lighten the mood.

It doesn't work.

"I need to study."

"You can study over coffee. Get some coffee with me. Maybe I can help."

She exhales a deep breath. "It's not a good idea. Please, just let me go home."

"I didn't know you want to be a lawyer."

Quinn looks away. "I don't want to talk about it. And please don't say anything to anyone."

I hold up both hands. "Okay, I promise. But let me take you to get a cup of coffee. I won't even bring it up."

She glares up at me. "You're not going to leave me alone until you get your way, are you?"

I shake my head and grin. No words need to be said.

"Ugh. Fine. But I mean it, Deacon, no being a jerk."

I widen my eyes and feign innocence. "I'm never a jerk." Grabbing her bag from the back seat, I lead her to my car and wonder how fast she's going to try to run when she realizes I'm taking her to my place. Better save that news for when she's buckled in the car. I didn't say where we'd be going and coffee at my apartment is the best.

One fact isn't lost on me. I never take women home. She'll be the first.

My place is just that—mine.

I don't want them randomly showing up or leaving their purse or jacket as an excuse to return. It's my lair and it's off limits to women.

Well, it was, it seems.

Quinn is different. The thought of taking her there makes me a little anxious, but I can't help myself.

When I open the passenger door, she sinks down in the seat and her skirt rides up a little on her thigh. My cock attempts to spring to life and I will it to go back down in my pants. Handing her bag off to her, I jog around the back of the car and fold myself into the driver's seat. Quinn's eyebrows shoot up when Dr. Dre's *The Chronic* blares from the speakers.

I look over at her, turning the volume down. "What?"

She shrugs. "Nothing. Just took you as more of an 80s hairband kinda guy. Expected Van Halen."

"Hmm. What kind of shit you listen to? Let me guess. Taylor Swift?"

"No thanks. I'm more of a Foo Fighters kind of girl."

I nod. "Not bad. Not bad. It's kind of punk rock." I drag out the last syllable and it gets a small smile out of her.

One small step for man…

I navigate into the late evening traffic. We pass three coffee shops.

Quinn notices, craning her head to follow each one as we drive by. "Where are you taking us? Canada?"

"It's a great spot. Trust me." I grin and place my hand on the upper part of her leg that's still covered. She doesn't push it away, and I smirk to myself.

One giant leap…

I'm tempted to inch my hand up farther, but I don't want to piss her off…not yet. I'm surprised she even got in the car and I take victories when I can get them.

We arrive outside my building and Quinn wheels around on me. "Is this some kind of joke? I might stab you with my pen."

I bug my eyes at her. "No need to be violent, damn. You'll appreciate the view, and I make a good cup of coffee." I flash her a smile to ease her temper.

She folds her arms across her chest. It pushes her tits together, and I have an unbelievable urge to dive head-first right into them.

"Didn't know you were capable of operating a coffee pot."

"There's more to me than my big dick."

Her cheeks flush pink at the mention of my cock.

It's adorable when I know how dirty she can be.

She smacks my chest with the back of her hand. "Damn it, Deacon. You said you'd behave."

"Oh, please. I'm a perfect gentleman." I exit the car and open her door, grinning my ass off. "It's just anatomy. No need to be shy."

QUINN

"MAKE YOURSELF COMFORTABLE. I'll get the coffee going." Deacon fumbles around his sleek, modern kitchen with stainless steel appliances. He looks clumsy in it, and I wonder if he's ever even made coffee before. It *is* nice to have him waiting on me for once. I've never seen him run his own errands, ever.

Moving through the apartment, I drop my bag on the kitchen counter. His place is the bachelor pad of all bachelor pads, and I wonder if I should sanitize my hands before I touch anything. Everything is oversized, from his giant television mounted on the wall to his black leather sofa that's large enough for three people to sleep on.

I explore the room more, taking in the decor. There are some black and white pictures of him with his brothers. It's when they were kids, and I can barely tell any of them apart. They all wear the same boyish grins on their faces.

I move down the line and there are a few pictures of him and Jenny, his niece. Decker's in a few of them. There are some signed Bears footballs that my dad would go nuts over. Walter Payton and Mike Singletary and Brian Urlacher. I shrug. I recognize the names and have heard them a million times, but that's about it. I'm not big into sports. I watch football with Dad on occasion because he loves it so much and we used to go to games when I was little.

The city slowly lights up below, building by building, as the sun fades over the horizon. Lake Michigan sits to the east and the pretty colors of the sunset play off the waters. Deacon was right about one thing. I do love the view. It's gorgeous. I stare out the floor-to-ceiling window that runs the length of his living room.

The smell of expensive coffee fills the air.

I guess he figured out how to make it. Good for him.

He approaches me from behind. "Be ready in a few minutes." He reaches around me. I'm so relaxed I start to lean back and stumble a little.

"Shit, Quinn." With cat-like reflexes, he catches me and for a long moment has me wrapped up in his arms. We linger for a bit before he stands me upright.

He snickers and reaches over to open a door that leads onto a small terrace.

God, I'm such a klutz around him.

The little balcony is beautiful. Large plants overflow from pots placed equidistant along the wall, and there are a couple huge lounge chairs.

I move onto the patio and take it all in. "Pretty breathtaking."

"Yeah, you are."

My stomach coils into a knot, and I wince internally at

the same time. I shouldn't be around him yet I can't stay away.

"I like to sit out here and drink coffee when I work from home."

"I can see why."

He moves past me and flips on the outside light. "Have a seat and get comfortable. I'll grab your bag. There's an ethernet hook-up if you need the internet, or the Wi-Fi password is KimJongTateSucks. No spaces. First letter of each word capitalized."

I shake my head at him.

He shrugs. "What?"

"Nothing. Thanks." I sink down in the thick cushions of one of the chairs and try to imagine Deacon sitting here, mulling over his cases. He returns minutes later with my bag and a steaming mug.

I take a whiff and breathe it in. My eyebrows shoot up. It's hazelnut creamer and two sugars. No wonder he was fussing with it for so long. "How'd you know to make it like this?" I smile over the brim, blowing on the hot liquid before taking a sip.

He takes a seat in one of the other chairs, but his gray eyes fix on mine. "I pay attention more than you think. I notice every little detail about you, Quinn."

My cheeks warm and I'm not sure if it's the coffee or the words coming from Deacon's mouth. Probably both. "I should study." I know it's rude to cut him off when he's being so nice but it's all too much. I'm overwhelmed just being here and I really do need to go over my notes.

"I'll leave you to it. Need to make a phone call." He gets up from the chair and walks back toward the door.

Much to my surprise, Deacon stays true to his word. He leaves me alone for nearly thirty minutes before returning to refill my cup. He takes the pot back to the kitchen and returns with a cinnamon roll that is to die for.

"Now, that's good." I let out a long moan because it's just that delicious.

"I love when you make that sound." His penetrating eyes heat me up from within. Brushing his thumb over my lips, he sweeps some crumbs from my mouth then licks them off.

God, it's so damn sexy. I know he wants me in his bed, and if I don't get out of here quickly, he's going to succeed.

I gather my stuff. Surprisingly, he doesn't try to stop me.

"I should go. You said you'd be on your best behavior. This test is important. This class is crucial for school."

"Umm, okay. Didn't realize I wasn't behaving." He shakes his head like he's confused. "You know the firm offers scholarships for this sort of thing. I could put in a good word for you. We'd pay for your degree."

I shake my head vehemently. It immediately becomes clear in my mind just how different our upbringings were and how many miles apart we are from one another. Or maybe I'm just searching for an excuse to get out of here before his little plan works on me. "I don't take handouts. I'm no charity case. I want to do this on my own for me. You don't understand what that's like because you're used to having everything handed to you." I pause and take a deep breath. He didn't really deserve that but it just kind of slipped out. "Look, Deacon. I'm not like you.

Where I come from you have to earn every damn thing you get."

His jaw ticks and he rubs his chin. I can see the intensity burning behind his steely gaze. I don't think he's ever been pissed at me before, but right now, the way he stares at me—he looks the part.

He doesn't explode, though. He sits there, calm. Almost mature, and I don't even know who I'm looking at now. It's like I'm finally staring at an adult.

"So, it's okay for you to just sum me up? Just like that?"

I shrink back in my seat a little. It's the closest we've ever had to a serious conversation and I'm in the wrong. It's unfamiliar territory.

Deacon stands up and paces toward the door. Now, the more the gears in his head spin, the more upset he looks. "Yeah, my life is so fucking easy. You know what it's like being Decker Collins' little brother? The baseball god. I could've been just as good as him, if not better, but I didn't want the pressure of living up to that. I loved baseball, but I played football just to spite him. Just to prove I could do something he couldn't. You think you know me, Quinn, but you don't. You don't even try."

I look down, unable to make eye contact with him.

He walks off toward the door but spins around at the last second. "I try with you. I try to be better. I've never done that for anyone. But I guess I'll never be more than some guy you fuck in the closet at work, right?"

His words are a slap across the face. It hurts—bad. The pain is almost unbearable because he's right. I've never really given him a fair chance. I've been hard on him and

73

maybe I did put him in a box and not bother to look deeper. Maybe the humorous side of him is a defense mechanism he uses to hide who he really is.

I walk over and reach for his forearm.

He won't look at me. I can tell I hurt him, and he doesn't want me to see it. Even now, I get the feeling he's not doing it out of shame. He's trying to protect my feelings, from seeing I've wounded him.

"I'm sorry. You're right."

He finally turns and faces me. "Right about what?"

"Everything you just said."

He leans down and places both palms on my cheeks and stares deep in my eyes. When he looks at me like this all my walls crumble down and I want to let him in. But I'm scared to put my trust in him. I'm scared to fall. Deacon Collins thrills and terrifies me at the same time. He has the ability to hurt me. We both know it. But he's so damn vulnerable right now. He's letting me in, and I get the feeling he's never let anyone else see him like this or told them the things he just told me.

"Look, I like you, Quinn. I don't know what I have to do to make you see that it's real."

Before I can speak, his mouth connects with mine and everything fades away.

Sliding his coffee-stained tongue between my lips, the man makes love to my mouth like he's practiced on me his entire life. Lowering to his knees, he slides a hand up my skirt, teasing his fingers over my panties, but he rests his cheek against my stomach. "I don't want to fight with you."

Instinctively, I reach out and pull him closer to me. I

bend down and whisper, "I know," against his jaw and move to unbutton his shirt.

He grabs my hand. "Slow down. We're not at work. We have plenty of time."

He's so sweet and intimate right now. I want it to last forever and at the same time I wish it was just another quickie so I wouldn't have to deal with all these new emotions swarming through me.

My mind races. Deacon makes me feel so damn dizzy and confused.

When we're about to kiss again, my phone buzzes from my bag and it breaks the spell between us. I pull it out and see my father's name light up the screen. "Shit. I gotta go. I'm sorry." I shove past him, nearly tripping over him as I rush to grab my things. My father expected me home an hour ago. He's probably worried.

"Quinn."

His word hits me in my back and I look over my shoulder to get one last look at him. I just want to see his face once more while he's fully exposed to me, showing me who he really is.

It's a mistake. The disappointment in his eyes burns a hole in my chest, but I just can't deal with this right now. I have too much going on with my dad and school.

If only circumstances were different. After everything he just told me, maybe we'd have a chance.

DEACON

A COLD SHOWER isn't enough to ease the pain after Quinn rushed out on me. I don't get her at all. She acts like I'm the one who plays games but she's yanking my strings like a fucking puppet master. I can't get her out of my head. The sugary taste of her lips. Her green eyes and auburn hair.

I completely opened up to her. I've never done that with anyone. It just sort of happened and all spilled out before I could stop it. That's the effect she has on me. But look what happened.

It's why I keep that shit bottled up inside. I hate harboring resentment, and I don't like to look weak. My whole life I've been told not to talk about my feelings. Suck it up and get the job done. Fucking around and joking keeps me from having to face the harsh realities of life and deal with that shit.

What I should do, is give up. But, I can't. I'm not a quitter and I know what the fuck I want.

Her.

I collapse on my bed and look at the clock wondering if she's awake and as horny as I am.

The woman drives me crazy. I want her here right now, next to me, in my arms. Not even necessarily to fuck her. I just love when she's around me, talks to me. Even if it's about real shit.

Yeah, there's no way in hell she's getting rid of me. I'm a persistent son of a bitch when I want something. She'll learn. She'll have dinner with me. I don't care if I have to back her into a corner and grind her down for years.

It's my mission. I'm starting to wonder if there's something wrong with me when it comes to her. I'm acting like a little bitch. It hurts when she constantly turns me down and tosses my flowers in the garbage. Especially when I know she wants me as much as I want her.

What's her fucking deal? If she'd just tell me, maybe I could move on, but she makes no goddamn sense.

At the same time, all of it only makes me want her more. She'll be mine.

I grab my cell phone off the nightstand and look at our last text exchange when she sent me the cleavage shot. It's hot as fuck but doesn't compare to the real thing. My finger hovers over the call button, and my cock grows harder at the thought of her voice and the way she feels when she trembles while I'm inside her. Fuck it. I need to hear her. Even if she yells at me.

"Why are you calling?"

"Why do you think?"

"Deacon…" My name trails away. She's warring with herself, I can tell.

Just talk to me, woman! Let me in that brain of yours.

"I'm trying to study."

"I need you."

"I'm not talking dirty to you over the phone. I'm sure you have a list of women on reserve." She pauses. "Sorry, I didn't mean that. I'm just…"

"No, you're not wrong. But none of them make me feel the way you do. You're the one that does it for me. There's nothing I love more than wrapping my hand around your throat while you come undone."

She breathes heavily into the phone and I make a fist around my dick.

"Come on. At least tell me what you're wearing."

"Fine. You want to know what I'm wearing?"

My cock hardens in my palm. Now, we're getting somewhere. "Hell yes."

"I just took a bath and shaved."

I fight back a groan. "Keep going."

"I shaved everywhere. Completely bare except for a little strip of hair and I can't stop running my fingers over my body wishing they were yours."

"I do believe I like the sound of that. You're pretty good at this." I pump my cock a couple times in my hand. "Keep going."

"Hmm…I want to drag my nails through your hair, pulling and pushing your head between my legs, shoving your mouth on me. I'm imagining your tongue licking me up and down, getting me nice and wet for you."

"God, I'm so close, Quinn." I can already feel a load of epic proportions building in my balls. I didn't expect her to talk so dirty over the phone.

"God, Deacon. You feel so good. I want you inside me right now. I'm using my fingers but it's not enough. I want you to take control. I need you inside me so bad." She lets out a loud moan, but it's too loud. It almost sounds like a shitty porn actress screaming while the dude fucks her.

"You're not really touching yourself, are you?"

She belts out a laugh. "No. I'm sitting here staring at my notes wearing an oversized nightgown, pink fuzzy bunny slippers, and a green mud face mask."

I let out a sigh of disapproval. "All wood gone. Totally deflated."

She giggles, clearly amused with herself, and it's ridiculously cute. "You brought it on yourself, sir."

"If you come over, I could probably tie a stick to it and still get it inside."

"Goodnight, Deacon." She dies laughing and the line goes dead.

My head falls back on my pillow and I stare down at my cock. "Just a minor setback, buddy. It won't stop us." I close my eyes and allow my thoughts to drift back to the fantasy she built moments ago. I imagine Quinn lying on her bed naked with her legs spread, stuffing her pussy with three fingers while thinking about my cock.

My dick rallies in my hand, hard once again.

Told you.

I stroke back and forth, until I'm fucking my hand so hard my arm slaps against my thighs. I'd sum it up as vigorous masturbation. The woman drives me nuts. Her moans play through my mind. I can see it now, a crystal-clear image.

I bet she's touching herself, wishing she hadn't hung

up on me. Her fingers are slick and she's thinking about riding me. Fuck. If I knew where she lived, I'd go over there right now and take what I want. If I was there, she'd give in. Quinn thinks she's pushing me away but she's only amping this situation up to eleven.

She knows that smart mouth of hers turns me on.

Sweat beads across my forehead. Quinn has me hot and bothered that's for damn sure.

God.

I let out a groan and jerk harder and faster, thinking about what it'd be like to come inside her, mark her as mine. Fuck, that's like my all-time fantasy rolled into one. Afterward, I'd pull out and put her down on her knees so she could clean her pussy off my cock with her tongue.

The vision loops through my head until I can't take it anymore. Hot spurts of come shoot up onto my stomach. I lie there, breathing heavily, hand all sticky.

I should get myself cleaned up, but just the thought of fucking Quinn totally wipes me out.

I've got it for this woman—bad.

QUINN

MY ALARM SOUNDS and I groan, covering my head with my pillow. I'm so not ready to get up and get this day started. The first part of my morning is spent getting Dad out of bed and into his chair so he can take care of his morning business. Our bathroom is handicapped accessible so that takes some stress off both of us. Once he's situated and I'm sure he doesn't need my help with anything, I start breakfast and get ready for work. I still have nearly two hours, but the time will fly. I know from experience.

Some days go smoother than others, depending on Dad's strength. On a great day he functions with little help but on a bad day, he can barely hold a cup of water. Today's a good day and I breathe a sigh of relief. A few times he's fallen out of his chair or nearly caught the apartment on fire trying to do too much on his own. He's truly as stubborn as they come.

He wheels himself out of the bathroom and slides into his spot at the table. I notice some small pieces of tissue where he tried to shave and cut himself.

"I could've helped." I motion toward his jaw as I plate his eggs and toast.

"I've been thinking, kiddo."

Here we go. I already know what's coming.

"Yeah? What's that?"

"I should move into one of those assisted living places. You've got enough to worry about without working so damn hard all the time to take care of my old ass. This isn't the life I want for you."

I smile. He brings this up at least once a week. "There's nothing I'd rather be doing. You need to stop. When Mom left, you could've dumped me off with the state. It would've been easier. But, you didn't."

"That's different. That was the best damn day of my life. You gave me purpose. Being your dad made me a better man."

I stand up and give him a peck on the cheek. "I love you, Dad. No more talk about you living in a home. Got it?" I point at him with a butter knife.

"Fine. Got it, kiddo. Breakfast is good." His hand trembles as he brings his mug to his lips, and I pretend not to notice. I hate that his health has declined so much these past few years.

"Thanks. Your lunch is in the fridge. Tuna sandwich and fruit salad." I finish my breakfast and rinse our plates in the sink. I glance at the clock and notice I'm making good time.

Before I leave for work, I get the television set up for him. He loves Classic Sports on ESPN and they're airing an old Bears game.

Some of my fondest memories are going to games with

him when I was a kid. His buddy Joe always went with us. God rest his soul. I know Dad misses him. I do too. They were like partners in crime. Not a single Sunday night passed by when they didn't go out for a beer and to watch a game, once I was old enough to stay home by myself. I worry about him getting lonely. It's been almost a year since Joe passed. He needs someone his age he can relate to.

I kiss him on the forehead and gather up my stuff. "I should be home for dinner tonight." I point a finger at him. "Stay out of trouble."

"Oh, don't worry about me. Just inviting over a few strippers and the Ronnie kid from down the hall. He has the best weed."

I shake my head. "Don't burn the place down. And no cigars!" I found his new stash hidden down in his recliner last week. Ronnie sneaks them in when I'm at work. Dad has all the neighbors on our floor wrapped around his finger.

As soon as I get to my car Heather calls to tell me about her wild night with Stewart.

"I think he might be the one."

I roll my eyes. "Every man is the one with you."

"Hey, some of us enjoy sex."

"I get plenty of attention. Don't worry about me."

"Is that where you disappeared to Saturday when you stood me up?"

"Got called into work." My cheeks flush thinking about how Deacon bent me over his desk and had his way with me. I wonder if he's pissed I left him hanging after our phone call.

"Is that what the kids are calling it these days?"

"Stop it. We're so not talking about this."

"Killjoy. We *will* talk about this. Soon. Over drinks. You should come by the store this Friday. We're having a big sale."

"Gotta go. I'm driving."

"Bye, bitch."

I drop my cell phone in the passenger seat and focus on the morning commute. I definitely don't think about Deacon Collins at all on the way to work.

DEACON

THE MOMENT I get off the elevator at work, Tecker awaits me with huge smirks on their faces. "Welcome back, professor." Decker snickers.

Tate gives me the evil eye. I swear, Decker needs to fuck her better because she always looks pissed off. It's sad too, because she can hurl insults with the best of them, and they're pretty damn funny.

"You'll be happy to know the lecture was a success. They liked me so much they invited me back next week."

Decker smiles like he's almost proud.

"The offer was later rescinded after I was caught with my pants down and the top student's lips wrapped around my... Well, you get the idea." I wink.

My brother's face hardens, and he narrows his gaze on me. "You better be fucking joking."

I love that he's not sure. I hold my hands up like I'm weighing something with an invisible scale. "Maybe I am maybe I'm not." I shrug. "That's what you want to hear, right? That it was a shitshow."

Asshole.

Truth be told, I crushed that presentation. Every student in that class will be applying at The Hunter Group when they graduate.

So Tecker can eat a shit pie.

I head toward my office as they go into the boardroom for a meeting with Cole Miller, and conference call with Weston Hunter.

Weston's the big swinging dick in Dallas who took over our firm. I shouldn't say he took over. They kept the name, but that's about it. We all work together in a large partnership. Weston is Tate's former boss and one of Decker's old friends.

Tate, God, that woman. We got along for a brief second, but I just find that I don't like her all that much. She's too intense. Her and Decker are a match made in heaven. I bet they sit around and go over their itinerary for the day in the mornings. Probably have a set schedule for every sexual position and have it mapped out to the second.

And my brother is going to marry her. He proposed once our merger with The Hunter Group was complete. I should try harder to get along with her, but she makes it difficult. She thinks she runs this firm and it pisses me off. We've built this thing for a decade and she acts like she can walk up in here and start bossing people around.

Fuck that.

She wasn't even a goddamn partner until the merger went through. When Decker started the firm, it was supposed to be something for us—the Collins brothers. Not the Collins brothers and Tate.

I get why he did it; for Jenny. Part of me is happy he gets more time with her, but we could've figured out a different way without bringing in some ass clowns from Texas. If he'd just sat us down and talked to us instead of making the final decision and ambushing us with it.

I do remember one thing, though. Decker fucked with me by sending me to the college. Thought he got one over on me.

That shall not go unchecked. It's just not my style.

Smirking to myself, I walk into his office and start messing with all his shit like I did when we were kids. I'd rearrange his toys and he'd damn near bust a blood vessel.

I go into Microsoft Office and change all the settings and fonts, then switch the language to Afrikaans. It's the first one I don't recognize. That'll take some time. I'm sure he didn't set it all up himself, so he'll need to get Quinn or someone from IT to fix it.

I plan to do enough damage it keeps him occupied half the afternoon. Once I'm satisfied with his computer, I turn the brightness on his monitor all the way down until his screen is black. His dumb ass will probably think it's not turning on. That'll occupy him for a bit until he figures it out, then he'll have to deal with all his settings.

Next, I start in on his desk and tape all his pens to the underside of his chair. He's going to fucking lose it.

I snicker to myself, mixing his paperclips and extra staples up after I empty the stapler. Yes, it's childish but I don't care. Serves him right for forcing me into that bullshit speaking engagement. Sure, I got to see Quinn out of the deal but that's beside the point.

Decker never takes me seriously. If he wants to treat me

like an annoying kid brother, that's how I'll behave. I eye a stack of files that look important and wonder how much shit I'd get in if they were misplaced. Sure, I'm an asshole but that might be pushing things too far and actually hurt a client. I leave them alone and move to his bookshelf instead, rearranging all the titles with the spines facing inward.

Finally finished, I survey my handiwork and smile to myself.

That'll do.

When I exit Decker's office, I spy Quinn at her desk talking to some guy with tattoos up his neck and down to his knuckles. I don't like the way he's looking at her.

Fuck, she looks hot as balls too. She's wearing a navy-blue skirt with a slit on the right side that teases at the lace tops of her thigh-highs.

I have to force down a groan and adjust myself when nobody is watching.

She smiles wide at the man and motions for him to follow her. My jaw ticks as jealousy spikes in my veins. It's a feeling I'm not used to, and one I don't like. I never get jealous. I already had a taste of it with that dipshit at the club, and I don't like it any more today. I never care if women I fuck see other people. Quinn isn't just any other woman, though.

As they near, I recognize the man now. Cole Miller, one of Dex's old buddies. He owns a chain of gyms and used to be a professional MMA fighter. He could probably kick the shit out of me. I wouldn't seek out a fight with him, and he's a client, but I don't give a fuck.

I'd die trying, if it came to that.

Quinn is mine and I don't appreciate the way he's eye-fucking her in that skirt. His gym is being sued in a huge body shaming case. Decker has been working around the clock on it. It's why he stuck me with those contracts for the Beckley brothers.

"Cole Miller, Deacon Collins." Quinn introduces us as she walks past me to get to Decker's office.

I exchange a quick handshake with the guy and his damn grip feels like it might crush a few bones. I don't wince at all, though. Because fuck him.

"They're in the boardroom." I nod toward the hall.

"Thanks." She shoots me a smile and turns to Cole. "If you'll give me a moment, I'll let Mr. Collins know you're here."

He smiles at me then stares at her ass as she walks away. My hands ball into fists at my sides. I want to tell him to wipe that fucking grin off his face, but I know I need to be on my best behavior. Decker really would fire my ass if I fucked this case up for him.

"Good luck with everything." My words come out through gritted teeth.

"Thanks."

I hang back and wait for Quinn to show him in. When she returns to her desk, she's all smiles, and it better not be because Cole was flirting with her.

"Have a hard time getting off last night after our phone call?"

I rub my jaw and grin. "Not at all." I lean in close and whisper in her ear, "Never came so hard in my life, but if you're still in need of some relief I'd be happy to help out.

It's getting close to lunch time and I'm starving." My lips brush the shell of her ear.

"Maybe you should get something to eat."

I whisper, "Your pussy is the only thing I'm hungry for."

By the way she just shivered a little at my words, I know I'll be meeting her in the supply closet soon, I just have one thing I need to take care of first.

RICK LAWRENCE, our firm's private investigator, knocks on the door to my office.

"Come in." I close out a few windows on my computer and stand to shake his hand.

If anyone can solve my problem, it's him. He might be the cockiest bastard I've ever met, and he's surrounded by the Collins brothers every day. That's saying something. He's early thirties and dressed in some tattered jeans and a Led Zeppelin stretch tee.

He takes a seat and kicks his feet up on my desk. That's how you know he's the best at what he does. Dude has the balls to walk around like he owns the place, and nobody says shit to him about it. He's a fucking magician and about to make my life a lot easier.

"What's up?"

"You know that case I'm dealing with? Flynn? The heart surgeon? Sexual harassment shit?"

"Yeah. Heard he gave some broad a slap on the ass and a 'well done.'" He smirks like he doesn't see anything wrong with that scenario.

I have to fight back a laugh at his nonchalant attitude. "Yeah, it's total bullshit, but it's all he said, she said at this point. What I need from you is to do a full background work up and tail her around. I want to know who she meets with, who she's friends with, everything. Dig hard on it, but don't let her know you're there."

"No problem. I'll be a fucking ninja."

"Perfect. This is top priority; put it ahead of everything else. I don't give a shit what any of my brothers say."

His eyebrows rise. I know exactly what the gesture means.

"Your cooperation will not go unnoticed." Usually, I hook him up with some tickets to the firm's suite at Soldier Field.

He leans in. "I need something a little different this time. Call it alternate consideration."

Interesting.

"What do you have in mind?"

"There's a lot of new Dallas pussy running around this place."

He may be the most misogynistic person I've ever met. "I may have noticed."

"I want first dibs on my choice, above Donavan and Dex."

Fuck, this might be more difficult than I thought.

"I'm not a damn pimp. Won't some football tickets work?"

Rick smirks. "Won't need any help from you. Just keep them out of my way. I can handle the rest. Trust me."

I don't doubt what he's saying. I've never seen him have a problem landing some ass.

"Did you have someone in mind?"

He slow nods. "Oh yeah. Mary."

"Magdalene? The new paralegal who reads a bible during lunch and wears long skirts?"

Rick leans back in his chair. "That's the one."

I shake my head. "Well, I think you're fine on that front. I've seen Dexter ogling Abigail nonstop, and neither of my brothers like to work to get laid. Mary's not really their type."

"Well then. Consider this little problem of yours taken care of."

"Perfect. Let me know as soon as you find something."

He stands up. "No problem. I'll get right on it, as soon as I'm done brushing up on a few bible verses." He tosses me a shit-eating grin. "I'll get out of your way. I know you have somewhere to be."

"Where's that?"

"Supply closet." He walks out the door.

I stare at the door where Rick just walked out, shaking my head.

How the fuck does he know everything?

That guy is a goddamn enigma.

QUINN

THE WORKDAY DRAGS by and Deacon and his not-so-subtle hints don't help matters. I can't get the thought of him going down on me out of my head. It's bad. The man has turned me into a sex addict. How does he know which buttons of mine to press nonstop? He's relentless.

It pisses me off but here I am checking the clock and fidgeting with my pen, knowing I should stay far away from him. My line buzzes with a call from Tate.

"We're taking Mr. Miller out to lunch. I expect it to be a while so if you have anything you need to do, take an extra thirty minutes."

"Um, yeah. Thanks."

Tate is nice.

I know Deacon and her butt heads a lot, but I like her. She's friendly and sometimes we go to lunch together. It's nice to see a strong female lawyer who doesn't take shit from the guys and can hold her own. I hope to be like her once I pass the bar. I can relate to her. She's been here for months and doesn't seem to be great at making work friends. I suspect it has more to do with people thinking she was a spy, and now, she's suddenly Decker's fiancée.

It doesn't bother me. I'm glad to see Decker happy. He's actually loosened up some since she arrived. Tate was exactly what he needed, and speaking of need... I'm in need of some relief.

I should be taking the extra thirty minutes to study but there's always tonight.

Let's see. Study or have Deacon's mouth on me?

The boardroom doors open. Tate smiles at me, and Decker and Mr. Miller follow her to the elevator.

Pulling out my cell phone, I fire off a text to Deacon.

Quinn: You have five minutes. No more.

I make a quick trip to the bathroom to freshen up and decide to mess with Deacon and take off my panties before he can steal them this time. I've bought more underwear these past few months than I have my entire life. I should hit him up for a gift card to Victoria's Secret the next time he wants to send me flowers. He owes me.

What the hell does he even do with them? Wait, I don't want to know.

By the time I get to the closet more than five minutes has passed and Deacon is waiting.

The irritated look on his face smooths into that devilish smirk of his. Those stormy grays narrow on me. "You're late."

He yanks me inside and shoves my chest flat against the wall, then pins me in from behind. The manly scent of his cologne wraps around me and I breathe him in.

He makes me crazy. I feel so wild and free in the moments we're together. When it's the two of us there are no expectations. No commitments. I'm not running here and there trying to keep up with life. I'm not a student or caregiver or, hell, even a friend. I'm simply me, and Deacon never fails to make me feel a whole lot better.

His mouth connects with my neck with such raw passion it nearly takes my breath away. He sucks at my throat, almost hard enough I'm worried he'll leave marks. I should fight against him, but I can't. I'm a slave to him as his hands roam down my legs and tug my skirt up.

"Thought you were cute with that performance last night, didn't you?"

"Deacon…I'm sorry about…"

"No, you're not." He removes his jacket and tosses it on the floor, then spins me around. "On your knees."

I glare back at him. "Thought you were having me for lunch?"

He shrugs. "Plans change. On your knees, Quinn."

God, he's so commanding.

I kneel in front of him.

When he unzips his pants, his thick cock juts out of his slacks.

Maybe it won't be so bad. He never fails to provide me with orgasms, so it really is only fair, and I don't mind. Licking my lips, I'm eager to taste him. Eager to please him. Gripping his cock, Deacon tilts his hips and feeds it to me slowly. I've only done this for him, but he doesn't know that.

The first time his size terrified me, but I got used to it. I love the sounds he makes when I put him in my mouth. Deacon is all alpha but when I go down on him, I'm the one in control. My lips wrap around the crown and I swirl my tongue along the tip, tasting and teasing him. His fingers dig into my scalp and hold my head in place. Flattening my tongue on his shaft, I take him deeper and suck until my lips stretch and burn to accept more of him. I bob up and down and gag when he begins to fuck my mouth.

"Fuck, Quinn." He groans.

I reach up with my hand and stroke the rest of him that doesn't fit. I may have watched some porn to try and learn how to do it better, after my first time with him.

He finally pulls back and stares down at me, breathing heavily with intense eyes. "You keep that up and this will be over faster than I want."

"You don't have much time left."

"Right." He reaches down and helps me up from my knees.

I watch him go through the motions of putting on a condom and nervously wait for what's to come.

DEACON

QUINN GLANCES over her shoulder at me. She's braced against the back of the supply room door, skirt shoved up to her stomach, her bare ass sticking out, ready and waiting.

Part of me frowns internally, wondering how much better it'd be if she'd at least let me take her someplace nice with a fucking bed. Not that the sex isn't good. It's fucking phenomenal, but she's better than this. I want more with her than to fuck in this closet.

I want to lay her down and take my time instead of being so damn rushed. Not that the thought of getting caught isn't a turn on. It definitely is.

Fuck, I can't stay away from her. I think about her all the time. When I wake up, I can't wait to get to the office just to see what she's wearing, and when I lie down at night, I don't think about fucking her at all.

I picture what it'd be like to take her out to dinner, hold her hand, and show her there's more to me than a childish bastard in a suit who plays games and fucks like a god. Her words not mine, to be fair.

I damn sure won't tell her I don't want to fuck her right now, though. That will never happen. I take what I can get. Stepping up behind her, I line up with her and glide right in because she's so damn wet.

"Fuck, that's nice." Gripping her hips, I slam into her, wishing I could feel her skin to skin. I never fuck without a condom but for her I'd take the risk, just for that deeper connection. I keep that thought to myself. One, because it scares the hell out of me to think like that and two, I don't want to run her off. I don't know when I went from lust to like, but I really like this woman. More than a little. More than a lot, even.

Quinn trembles under my touch when I slide a hand around her waist and stroke her clit.

"Oh, shit." She lets out a whimper, and I cover her mouth to muffle her moans.

I wish I could see her on top of me just once. Lack of space has never permitted her to ride me. I'm tempted to throw her over my shoulder and take her to the couch in my office. Watch her breasts bounce while she grinds on my cock.

There's an old folding chair in the corner. The gears in my brain start to turn. It might just work.

I want to see her face when she comes. As I pull out, she gives me an evil eye. A look that might kill lesser men. I unfold the chair and sit down, holding my cock straight up.

Quinn saunters toward me and she's like all my fantasies rolled into one with each sway of her hips.

Lowering herself to my lap she eases herself down onto me, gripping my shoulders. Her tits rub up against my chest, and I love every second of her pressed to me—as close as she can get. She kisses me with an intensity I've never felt before. I'm getting to her. Inch by inch, I know I am.

Hips grinding, bodies rocking, we fuck fast and hard. She bounces up and down as her ass claps on my thighs. The only things passing between us are heavy breaths and stifled moans. Her eyes burn a hole into my retinas. Clenching her muscles tight, she shivers and shakes, mumbling my name against my neck.

I fist a handful of her hair and tug her head back. "Eyes on me when you come."

Once she rides out her orgasm, she looks sated and completely spent. I smack her ass, trying to bring her back to the present, and order her to bend over the counter.

Quinn may have come already, but I haven't. Not that I'm too far behind, though. I'm so damn close. What I want is to rip this condom off and really feel her, but I don't. I shove into her from behind and fuck my frustrations out. A tremble starts in my legs and my balls lift and tighten. I try to hold back as long as I can, but the intensity is too much as the orgasm inches up my shaft.

All I can say is, "Fuck, Quinn," as I blow into the condom.

The whole time I imagine what it'd be like to come inside her. The thought of marking her as mine overwhelms me.

It's an obsession.

One day.

After a few moments of heavy breathing, we both look at each other and smile. Fuck me. I don't know how I'm supposed to go back to work after that.

I feel like a little bitch, because all I want to do is hold her in my arms and sleep. Then fuck her again when I wake up, of course. I've never felt this way with anyone. I've never wanted much of anything until Quinn came along. She makes me feel like I can take over the world. Makes me want to be better for her.

QUINN

WHEN TATE INVITED me to lunch at The Capital Grille, I couldn't say no. I should be studying for my test, but this place is amazing and I'm starving. I was slammed all morning with the Cole Miller case and running errands for Donavan because his secretary called in sick.

"You've been quiet lately." Tate picks at the olives in her salad.

"Just have a lot going on." I sip my water and hope she sticks to talking about her. "Haven't seen you much since you got that giant rock on your finger."

Tate flashes her ring at me and smiles. "It *is* nice, isn't it?"

I nod. "It's gorgeous. Have you set a date?"

"No. We can't even agree on a location right now. My family's in Texas, but Decker's family is here. Well, his parents are in Florida, but all the brothers." I don't miss the disdain in her voice when she mentions the Collins brothers.

It's almost Shakespearean how none of them get along.

I take a piece of bread and slather it with butter. "Jenny still cool with you?"

She leans back and grins. "We get along great. Have a lot of fun going shopping on the weekends. Decker's credit card on the other hand...not so much."

"I can imagine."

"What about you?" She leans in, staring hard, but grins as she speaks. "Anybody special in your life?"

I look up and away before I catch myself. I shrug and try to play it off. "Just my dad." It's not a lie. I'm not dating Deacon.

"Dad sending you all those flowers?"

I swear she gets off on interrogating me. I shake my head. "Nah. Some guy who can't take a hint."

"We have a new employee coming up from Dallas. Well, I've known him for years, but he'll be new here. I could set something up."

My cheeks redden and I wonder what Deacon would think of that. "Isn't that against company policy? I don't mean you and Decker obviously but..." God, I want to shove my foot in my mouth.

She tucks a golden curl behind her ear and shrugs. "It's fine as long as he's not your superior and it doesn't get in the way of work. Technically, you work for Decker and well, he's taken." She leans in and lowers her voice. "The latest rumor around the office is either Deacon or Dexter has been taking someone in the supply closet for some extracurricular activities. Would you know anything about that?"

Shit.

My face has to be white as a ghost, but I shovel some food in my mouth and shake my head. "I don't pay attention to those clowns."

Tate grins, and I know she sees right through my bullshit. The woman can read any situation. "You'll keep an eye out and let me know if you see anything? Last thing we need is trouble because those idiots can't keep it in their pants."

"Absolutely." I nod.

This lunch can't end soon enough.

BY THE TIME I get home from my exam, Dad's already asleep. I clean up the remnants of his dinner and tidy the apartment up a little. I crushed my test and feel like a huge weight lifted from my shoulders. I can breathe easy for a bit, until the next one.

Heating up some leftovers, I curl up on the couch and channel surf. I can't remember the last time I watched TV. Ironically, I feel like my only down time is spent with Deacon, which is ten minutes here and there. Even when I tried to go out with Heather, I ended up with him. I know it's pathetic, but the second I think about him, I have this urge to call and tell him about my test. He's the only person I know who can relate and knows I'm going to law school. I should be exhausted, but I'm wired after dumping all that information from my brain. Sleeping is not an option at the moment.

I pull up Deacon's number as I walk to my bedroom, and I'm torn. Should I call him? I want to so damn bad, but I'm not sure it's the greatest idea.

After a quick battle with myself, I collapse onto my bed and hit the send button. He answers on the third ring, and I hope I didn't wake him up.

"What's up?" He doesn't sound tired at all.

I'm not sure if I should be happy or if it should bother me. Is he out with someone? I shouldn't feel jealous. I don't even know if he is, but it's all my brain can focus on. There's only one way to find out.

"Hopefully your dick."

He clears his throat, loud, and doesn't fire back any sarcastic remarks or play along.

Like an idiot, I continue. "Just got home and was thinking about the supply closet yesterday when I had you in my mouth. I was so damn wet."

I'm about to ask why he's so quiet when I hear a woman's voice in the background. "Sir, your table's ready. Will your date be joining you soon?"

"Quinn, I'll have to call..."

"Don't bother." I end the call and bite back the rage building in my chest.

I shouldn't even be upset, and I feel dumb for being hurt when I don't even know what he's doing or who he's with. Not to mention, I knew who Deacon was when we started up this little fling. This is exactly why I've turned him down every time he's asked me out. Still, I can't help the way I feel right now.

Stupid feelings.

Stupid Deacon.

Stupid supply closet.

No more.

I can't go there again with him.

I won't do it to myself.

DEACON

I STARE DOWN at my phone when Quinn hangs up.

What the hell just happened? She didn't even let me finish.

I glare at the hostess for using the word 'date' to describe this meeting, but I know it's not her fault.

Still, I don't even think Quinn heard it and she can't be that pissed off if she did. I'll just tell her what really went down later and everything will be fine.

Karen Richardson called when I left the office and asked to meet. She's the asshole employee in Cole Miller's lawsuit who took the photographs and posted them online. I almost told her to piss off, but maybe she has information I can pass along to Decker, if I can pry it out of her. There's no way in hell I'd ever represent her, but maybe this can get Tecker off my ass.

When she walks in, every male head in the restaurant turns in her direction. She's one of those women who looks like a knockout from far away. She has huge fake tits and probably a plastic ass to match it, platinum blonde hair, tight mini skirt. You know the deal. Up close there's not a natural thing on her body, skin all shiny and stretched across her face.

I turn to the hostess. "Hold on, I think that's her."

She walks up. "Deacon Collins?"

I nod and shake hands with her.

We follow the hostess through the crowded bar to a private table in the back. It's a walled booth with a table and a chair on the other side. I take the booth because I'm Deacon Collins and I like to be comfortable. The crazy bitch slides in next to me.

What the fuck?

My mind immediately flashes to Quinn and my stomach ties in a knot, knowing what she'd think if she saw this. I shake myself from my thoughts, because I need to see if this chick has any information we can use.

Once we order drinks, she snuggles right into my side and it's painfully obvious this woman is coming on to me.

Every other man in the restaurant is probably jealous as shit right now, and until a few months ago, I'd be totally open to this. But not now.

I have to get the hell out of here.

I slide away from her, trying to create some kind of separation between us. "What can I do for you, Ms. Richardson?" Maybe she'll take the hint when I use her last name.

She makes a show of flipping her hair. "I didn't mean for things to get so out of control. Haven't you ever done something you regretted?" She flutters her fake lashes at me.

I want to tell her yeah, I know exactly what she means,

like agreeing to meet her for drinks. I can already tell this is a waste of time. Maybe I can salvage something out of it to pass off to Tecker, though. "What was your intention when you posted the photos?"

"It didn't start out malicious. I was taking selfies at work and that cow just happened to be in the background reflected in the mirror. I didn't notice her at first, but my girlfriends pointed it out to me, and we had a laugh. It was just a joke. I don't see what the big deal is. It was harmless. I know I should've taken them down the minute she saw them, but my post was getting so many likes and shares. It felt like I was famous until my account got shutdown and everyone turned on me." She leans in close and presses her cleavage damn near on my arm. "I called you because I'm hoping you can sell the rights or something. I don't know what it's called. Maybe I can get some sort of movie deal out of this. I'd look good on TV, don't you think?"

This woman might be the biggest dipshit I've ever met.

Not only does she want a movie deal out of what she did, she called the fucking attorneys representing her former boss. Her hand on my thigh is a clear indication of exactly what she's willing to do to get it.

I push down the rage building in my chest, and somehow manage to politely remove her hand from my leg. All I can think about is Quinn and how pissed she would be if she saw what was happening.

"Do you practice entertainment law? We'd look great together in the media. I looked up your brother and saw he's engaged but you're better looking anyway."

Part of me is so shocked at this woman, it makes it

difficult to stand up and get the fuck out of here. I glance at my watch and down the rest of my drink, trying to play it cool before I make my escape because she's clearly a stage five clinger.

"Do you think Cole would want to team up?"

Is she serious? Cole fired her. "No."

She frowns.

I bite back all the shit I want to say to her. "I apologize, but I won't be able to help you. Good luck, though." I walk from the table without looking back. I don't want to turn around and give her some reason to come chasing after me.

The minute I'm out the door, I already have Quinn's number pulled up. We need to talk. I have to tell her how I feel and make her understand, because I can't keep these emotions in check. She keeps sending me to voicemail and it's really starting to piss me off. If I knew her address, I'd drive straight to her damn house.

———

QUINN DIDN'T RESPOND to any of my calls or texts all night long or this morning. The second I walk in the office I search for her. She isn't at her desk or in the breakroom. I even check the freaking bathroom. She's clearly going out of her way to avoid me.

Is she that pissed off?

Surely not, but it makes me even more determined to find her. She's going to talk to me one way or the other. When I get to my desk, I call and order her flowers and two boxes of chocolate this time.

It's Friday after all. Some traditions are sacred.

She might throw them away, but she can't hide that quick smile that lights up on her face every time.

She's permanent relationship material. The kind of woman you take home to meet the parents. I never thought I could do the serious thing, but she's it. Deep down, I've known all along. I can't stop thinking about it—about her. Non-stop, twenty-four seven, on a fucking loop, Quinn on the brain. Taking this to the next level is my only option because I can't see myself ever not wanting to be with her.

On my way to lunch, I finally catch her at her desk but the second she sees me she bolts from her chair.

Part of me is flustered, but I'm a competitive son of a bitch. It only fuels the fire.

Two can play this game. Does she really think she can avoid me forever? I pull out my phone and put my plan into action.

Check mate, Quinn.

QUINN

A NOTIFICATION from Outlook pings on my phone.

What the hell?

I open it and the bright red letters jump out at me. It's a meeting request with Deacon and it's marked urgent. It has the exclamation point and everything.

He doesn't set up meetings. I can't believe he even figured out how to work the damn thing.

My face heats up and the hackles on the back of my neck rise. It's just like him to abuse his authority to get his way.

If I don't show for the meeting he could go to Decker and get me in trouble for insubordination. I wouldn't put it past him to make up some reason why he needs to meet and make me look bad for not responding.

The worst part is he knows me damn near as well as I know myself. When I have something on my schedule, I *have* to check it off. It's one of my biggest pet peeves; tasks lingering and not closed out. I grind my teeth as I hit accept on the meeting.

He's a jerk.

THE TIME for us to meet rolls around, and I march into his office—on time—to give him a piece of my mind.

"Shut the door and have a seat." He speaks before I can get a word in and it flusters me even more.

The smug bastard grins from behind his big desk. Man, he looks powerful in his Saint Laurent three-piece suit.

Stay focused.

I remain standing and look away from him just so his smoldering gaze won't get to me. My brain already spent the entire night cursing him, then trying to reason away what he was doing. In a rare turn of events, the part of my brain that tried not to hate him seemed logical. I didn't give him a chance to explain and I should have. I never jump to conclusions about things, except when it comes to Deacon. In fact, I hate when people do it.

After a long self-debate, I realized I was searching for a reason to end things with him, so I wouldn't get hurt. This is the perfect opportunity for it, and I'm not sure when another one might present itself.

"About last night…"

"Save it for someone else." I fold my arms across my chest and shake my head. His lame excuses make no difference—that's what I tell myself—and yet part of me wants to hear every last word. Instead, I convince my brain I deserve better and I'm not going to settle for some asshole player who might screw half of Chicago.

Nothing he says will change my mind. This was good

while it lasted, but it can't continue. We need to quit while we're ahead.

Deacon takes a step toward me, reaching for my forearms. "Will you just calm down for two goddamn seconds? Last night when you called, I was in a meeting. It was work related."

Did he just tell me to calm down? Does he not know a damn thing about women?

I yank my arms back. "Sorry, am I being too *hysterical* for you, Deacon?"

He must realize he said the wrong thing, because his eyes widen when he sees the scowl on my face.

I hold up my hand and take a deep breath. "You know what? It's fine. You aren't my boyfriend. You don't owe me an explanation."

"Look." He holds up a notepad as if it's supposed to mean something to me.

God, why can't he just let this go? Why does he have to be so focused on me?

"I was meeting with Karen Richardson."

I didn't realize it was possible to scowl harder than I already was, but I pull it off somehow. Was that supposed to make me feel better? I know who that woman is and what she looks like. Our firm has no reason to meet up with her for business. We're representing Mr. Miller. There's only one reason Deacon would be out with her so damn late. I wasn't born yesterday.

This seals the deal. I convince myself this is the chance I've been looking for to put all this shit in the rearview mirror. Maybe if I make it seem like it was my fault, it'll ease his conscience and he'll finally move on. "Look,

Deacon. It's okay, really. We had a good run. It was fun until it wasn't. I've been reckless and stupid to let it continue. It's my fault for letting it go on this long. It was bound to end in disaster so let's just rip the band aid off before it gets any more complicated. Please?"

As I speak, he stands up and pours himself a glass of water at a side table, ignoring my question.

I stand there, waiting for him to say something, but he doesn't. Finally, I nod. "All right, then. Good chat. I'm just going to go…" I trail off when he still doesn't reply and head toward the door.

Right when I'm a few feet from freedom, he grabs my hand and spins me around.

Shit.

Now, his back's to the door blocking my path. "We're not done here."

My pulse hammers at the sight of him. I don't know if I've ever seen his stare this intense. A storm rages behind his gray eyes, and I think I might drown in it. He doesn't even look mad, he's just so—serious.

I expect his eyes to rake up and down my body like they normally do, but they stay locked on mine. He doesn't even blink. "Nothing happened with that idiot last night."

I nod, but it's obviously fake. "Okay."

"You want the truth. I'll give it to you. She called and wanted to meet. I thought maybe I could get some information that could help the Miller case, so I could get Tate and Decker off my ass. That woman slid in next to me in a booth, and the only thing that went through my mind was, 'What if Quinn saw me like this?' And I got the fuck out of there as fast as I could and tried to call you back."

I know he's telling the truth, but this is my one opportunity to stop this madness before it escalates into a situation that hurts me. "You don't owe me an explanation."

"Why can't you just admit this is real between us?"

I feign ignorance. "I, umm…what are you talking about?"

"Stop denying it. You want me to kiss you—right now."

Yes, I want it so damn bad, but we have to end this. "No, I…"

"Bullshit. It's the only fucking thing going on in that head of yours and you hate yourself for it. I have no clue why you're fighting this, but you are." He leans in close, so close I feel his warm breath in my ear. "And if I put my hand up your skirt, we both know what I'd find. Your pussy, wet."

"You're an asshole." I spit the words at him.

The insult doesn't stop his mouth from crashing down on mine, turning my legs into nothing but trembling support beams that could give out any second. For a moment, my weakness almost wins out.

Almost.

Instead, I turn my head, separating our mouths. "Get out of my way."

Deacon's eyes burn into my retinas, but his mouth forms that cocky smirk of his, like he knows something I don't, and he nods lightly. "Okay." He steps out of the way. "I'll give you space for now."

As I walk past him, he leans down to my ear. "But nothing has changed. I *will* have you."

DEACON'S WORDS still ring in my head as I get out of my car and walk down the street to Heather's store. It sends a shiver up my spine just thinking about his voice, and goosebumps pebble down my arms.

My stomach tightens into a nervous knot thinking about what he said to me on my way out.

"Nothing has changed. I will *have you."*

The authority in his voice, and the way he said it—ugh, why can't I stay away from him? There was no mistaking his tone. He meant every last damn word of it. Why does he have to be so—Deacon? It's freaking hot and drives me nuts at the same time, not in a good way. How dare he act like he'll have me? What? Like he'll own me? Is that all I am to him? Some possession, like a toy he can take out and play with whenever he feels like it?

He says he wants a serious relationship, but does he really know what he's asking for? Not to mention, I don't have time for something like that. I just don't. Even if I wanted to give him a chance, I can't make that commitment right now. Even if he's capable of it, which I'm not convinced he is, it's still not possible.

I'm so damn confused, and I hate being confused. I like my life simple. A plus B equals C. Easy and clean. Black and white.

Deacon Collins muddies the waters. Everything is a gray area with him. Part of me is all for it and part of me wants to scream at the top of my lungs.

I could really use some girl talk. Hence, why I'm

waiting for Heather to get off work and gathering up the nerve to tell her about my secret fling with Deacon.

Keeping all this in for so long has made me crazy. She's going to be upset I hid it from her, but I hope she'll get over it quickly because I really need her right now. Hopefully, she'll understand, because she knows I like to keep my private life, well, private.

Heather must spot me debating with myself in front of the store. I don't even notice her until she's up in my face, going in for a hug. "Hey. I've missed you." She practically glows as she wraps her arms around me.

That glow can only mean one thing, she's falling for Stewart. He's so wrong for her, but what can I say, really? I've been banging my boss's brother for months. I'm not exactly Dr. Drew.

"Yeah, I had the big test."

"That's right. How'd you do?"

"They're posting grades tomorrow, but I'm pretty sure I nailed it."

"Knew you would. We should go for drinks to celebrate."

"Sounds perfect."

"Let me clock out and grab my purse." Her eyes light up. "Oh, my God. We should do karaoke at the bar down the road. I'll text Stewart."

I roll my eyes when she's not looking. So much for girl talk. I don't want to rain on her parade but hanging out with Stewart is the furthest thing from fun I can imagine. If she tells him I'll be there, Carter will show up too. I don't know if I can handle this, but I go along with it anyway.

She heads inside and returns with her bag. "You

hungry? They have appetizers, I think."

I nod. "Sure."

We walk a few blocks down to the bar. A sign out front reads KARAOKE 24/7.

My stomach growls as soon as the fried food smells waft into my nose. After the stressful week I've had I'm game for grease and alcohol. Between the shit with Deacon and worrying about my test I feel like I've been through the wringer.

Thunder rumbles above and a few raindrops plop on my head. It has to be an omen. We make a run for it and manage to dodge the incoming storm. Once we're inside the bar, I duck into the bathroom and dry off with a few paper towels. I remove the mascara from my eyes while Heather grabs us a table. After touching up my makeup, I run my fingers through my tangled hair to prevent knots. My phone pings with a text from Deacon, but I hit delete without even reading it.

Jerk.

I don't know why I let him get to me the way he does.

Because he's hot and funny and relentless.

Shut up, brain.

I fire off a quick text to Dad, so he doesn't worry when I'm not home at my usual time. Now that my reflection in the mirror borders on presentable, I shove my phone in my bag in case Deacon decides to call. I don't want to be tempted to answer.

I walk out and find Heather sitting at a table near the karaoke stage waiting on me with a pitcher of Bud Light and a basket of fried cheese sticks.

"Just us tonight. Stewart's working."

She frowns.

Secretly, I breathe a huge sigh of relief. "Good," I mumble where she can't hear and shove a cheese stick in my mouth. It's like heaven and I must look like I'm enjoying myself too much.

Heather tenses up but she doesn't say anything.

It's probably a good thing because if she starts in on me, I might say something I'll regret. I don't want to argue with her about how ridiculous men are, and I don't want to hear how amazing Stewart is because he's this week's boyfriend. I just want to enjoy myself.

It's not like I can really say much, anyway. This is who Heather is. She's a romantic, always falling hard and fast. I've known that since we were young, so I shouldn't expect anything else from her.

Before long, the topic of conversation shifts to work and school, and we're laughing and cutting up like usual.

I down one beer after another, drinking much faster than I should.

It just feels so good once it hits my lips.

Wow, quoting Old School? Slow down.

The happy hour crowd files in and the music starts up. After a few rounds, we make our way onto the stage to sing every single girl's anthem. *Truth Hurts* by Lizzo.

Heather shakes her ass while I belt out the lyrics. I'm positive I sound much better to myself than I do to everyone else, but who cares? This is exactly what I needed. To cut loose and forget about the world and all my problems for a bit.

Until I have to face Deacon tomorrow at work, anyway.

DEACON

I LEAVE a note with the flowers and chocolate.

If I find these in the trash there'll be two dozen next Friday along with a mariachi band.

-D

I move down the hall and wait for her to arrive. Watching her reaction is the best part, and I never miss it. I peek around the corner when she drops her bag into the bottom drawer of the desk like she always does.

She eyes the flowers and chocolate but doesn't touch them. I watch while she picks up the note. She scans over my handwriting, her lips moving as she reads the words to herself. Her eyes widen and she stares down at the trash can next to her desk.

You don't have it in you, Quinn.

Her lips curl up into a smile, just for a split-second, before a scowl returns.

You're mine and you know it.

She doesn't toss the flowers in the trash. But even if she had, it would've been worth it to see that smile.

It may have been short-lived, but she cares. She feels this between us and she's cracking. I'm wearing her down and I'll win her heart one way or another. I wait for her to head for the breakroom to make coffee. Her routine is so predictable. She's a creature of habit and I'm not above using any intelligence I've gathered over time to my advantage.

The second I spot those peep-toe heels turn the corner, I grab her hand and pull her into the closet. *Our* closet. The place where it all began.

"What the hell are you doing?" She snarls at me and fuck if I don't love the fire in her eyes.

I move in front of the door and lock it before she barrels her way past me.

"You do know what the word 'no' means, don't you?"

"Sure, but we both know it's not a real 'no.' Is it?" I smirk at the way her chest heaves with each breath she takes.

"This is kidnapping. I could scream."

I shrug. "You could, but you won't."

"I really hate you sometimes." Her green eyes blaze a hole in my chest.

"Get your hormones in check, woman. I didn't bring you in here to fuck."

Her eyes widen and then zero in on me. Her brows draw inward. "Do you even listen to the things you say? And why else would you pull me in here?"

I'd be lying if I said I didn't feel like an asshole because she thinks all I want is to put my dick inside her.

The moment gets to me and I freeze up for a few

seconds. This unfamiliar feeling gnaws at my stomach, like anxiety times a thousand, coupled with butterflies.

"Well?" She shakes her head like she's gathering her thoughts. "Why am I here?"

You can do this, Deacon.

"I have a question."

"Well, hurry. I'm running behind."

She's not running behind. She's always early for everything, but she has to stick to her routine, or it'll ruin her day. Like I said, I know every damn thing about her.

I suck in a breath. I don't know why this is so goddamn hard, and why I'm suddenly acting like such a pussy. My palms grow clammy and I exhale a long breath.

"Spit it out."

"I know you had a big test the other day and knowing you, I'm sure you killed it. I want to take you to dinner to celebrate."

Fuck, why was that so difficult?

"You sound sincere. Did you just formally ask me out on a date? A *real* date? Like a sit down at a restaurant and talk kind of date?"

"Look, I feel awful about the other night. I want to make it up to you. And I want to hear about your test and…" I fidget with my hands as I trail off and finally have the courage to look her in the eye. "Please?"

Quinn smiles, like she's enjoying this. "You're pale. You look scared shitless." She laughs like she's one part nervous one part elated. "Have you ever asked anyone on a real date before? One where you want to spend time with someone and not because you just want to get laid at the end?"

"No."

Her cheeks turn bright pink.

"I mean not like the way I just asked you. All formal or whatever." I shake my head at myself because I'm acting so ridiculous and flustered. "Fuck, I've never faced rejection before. This shit must be terrifying for normal guys. Doing this all the time."

She grins. "And he's back."

I snicker for a moment, but then narrow my gaze on her. "Look, I don't know how many more ways I can say this, for fuck's sake, but I like you. I've been up front about that from the beginning, and doing this kind of shit isn't easy for me, but I do it because I want you." I step in close, so that we're face to face, and trace her jaw with my finger. "What the hell do I need to do for you to see I mean every word? You think I've sent women flowers before? I don't even send my mother flowers."

She glances away, and I swear I think I might see a tear forming at the corner of her eye. When she turns back, it's gone. "I don't…"

"Stop fucking thinking. Tonight is happening."

QUINN

I FINALLY NOD MY HEAD.

Apparently, that appeases Deacon, because his mouth crashes into mine before I can utter a word. His kiss is different this time. It's not needy and rushed. He doesn't kiss me like he wants to consume me or turn me on. It's gentle and sweet, and I still don't know how to process any of this. He asked me out on an actual date. Not some, "Hey, let's hang out later," after he's done fucking me. And he said it was the first time he's ever asked someone out. I would normally think he was lying about the last part, but I could see the truth in his eyes.

The way he's kissing me is unexpected but nice. When his hand slides to my hip, I know my clothes are about to come off. My whole body warms under his touch and butterflies swarm my belly. I wait for him to strip me naked and shove me against the wall. Flip me around and spank me. Something.

But, he doesn't.

He pulls away, unlocks the door, and starts to walk out.

I glance back and forth, like someone might be coming. "Where the hell are you going?"

He shrugs. "Back to work."

I feel like I'm in *The Twilight Zone*. "Well, we're already in here and it's pretty obvious this is a sure thing." I stare at him like *seriously, you're passing up sex.*

His nostrils flare as he rakes his gaze up and down my body, and it looks like he's debating with himself. Finally, he runs a hand through his hair and frowns. Did I say something wrong? What's his deal?

My pulse races when he storms toward me like a man on a mission. I've never been so confused in my life. Is he going to have his way with me or not?

At the last second, he stops and bends down so we're at eye level. "I won't fuck you in this closet again. I want more, and you deserve better." He brings my knuckles to his lips. "This is real. See you tonight."

I exhale a huge breath I didn't realize I'd been holding and can't seem to find any words as he exits the closet. My body is on fire, my face flushed, and my eyes dart around the room.

What the hell just happened in here?

A small part of me saddens as I look around. If Deacon meant what he said, our exciting closet trysts are finished. I wait a few minutes and grab a stupid pen to cover my ass even though we didn't do anything wrong this time.

My heartbeat drums in my ear and my palms are slick with sweat. My body aches with need after not getting my usual release. I can still feel his intense eyes on me, like he's here, somewhere, staring at me, and every word of what he said replays through my mind.

Eventually, I let out a long exhale, and work up the courage to walk back into the office. The moment I turn the corner, Tate stands there waiting for me.

Her eyes flash to the pen in my hand. "Roof deck. Let's have a chat."

"Umm. Okay." I follow her outside and take in the view of Lake Michigan, still gripping the pen in my palm.

Tate smiles at me over her shoulder. "Get everything you needed back there?"

"Hmm?" I could plead ignorance, but Tate is smart... too smart for me to lie.

Fortunately, she moves on before I can answer. "You didn't throw away the flowers today. Finally give in to the guy who can't take no for an answer?"

"Not exactly."

"You know, I like to think of us as friends. You can talk to me. I know I can be a bit brash. I have to be that way to handle all the egos in this place. I won't run to Decker and throw you under the bus. Out here we're just friends. I promise."

I decide to be honest. I don't want to dig a hole for myself, and I have to get the words out before they consume me from within. Plus, if anyone can relate to dating one of the Collins brothers, it's Tate. As soon as I open my mouth the floodgates open.

For some reason, I can't look at her while I speak. "The flowers are from Deacon."

Tate grins. "I know."

I hang my head in shame, unable to look at her. "How?"

"Remember that time we went to brunch? You

131

mentioned a freckle on his thumb. You only know something like that about someone if you're, well, you know."

"I know he seems immature, but he just turned me down for sex and wants to take me on a date."

Tate let's out a laugh that's a partial gasp. "Did he now?"

I nod.

She mouths the word, "Wow," and puts both hands on her hips. "Well, maybe there's hope for that little shit stain after all. This could be good. Maybe you'll turn him into a functioning adult."

I laugh. "I don't know if *that* will ever happen, but maybe a slightly improved version of him."

"Truer words have never been spoken."

We both laugh for a second. It's hard not to smile at Deacon's boyish nature, even if it's annoying a lot of the time.

"Look, Quinn. All I ever cared about was my career and earning the respect of my peers. A relationship, let alone a marriage, was never really in the cards. But if I've learned one thing since I came to Chicago, it's that anything is possible." She looks down at her diamond engagement ring. "Deacon would be lucky to have you. And as much as it pains me to say this, he's right. You are worth so much more than a quickie in a closet. Make him earn you. *All* of you."

I glance out at the boats in the harbor, then on to the horizon of Lake Michigan. "I'm afraid to get my hopes up. In my experience, this usually plays out the exact opposite. The guy appears to be sweet and caring, but all his actions point the other way. With Deacon, he seems like a player. It's how I perceive him. But all his actions point the other direction, when I really step back and look at them. He's always been honest and up front. He tries to share intimate details with me. He pays attention to everything I enjoy, and not just when it comes to sex. He's sent me flowers every week since the first time we hooked up. He confuses me so much."

"Well I do think he likes you." She pauses for a second and glances around. "This stays between us." She leans in close and lowers her tone. "I personally don't think he's a great attorney." She straightens back up. "*But*, I do think he's a good person."

I want to believe she's right. I want to believe it so damn bad; the part about him being a good person and liking me.

"Now, get back inside. We have work to do."

When I arrive at my desk I can't focus on anything. All my thoughts keep going to Deacon and, if I'm being honest, what I'm going to wear tonight.

I shoot a text to Heather.

Quinn: Emergency. I need a new dress. Got a hot date.

Heather: Done. Come by the store. I know just the one.

I was so excited about Deacon I completely forgot to check my test score. I log into the student portal at the university and wiggle in my seat. When I see my score, I let out a squeal that earns me a few dirty looks from some of the employees passing by, but I don't care.

I aced it. Ninety-eight percent.

The weirdest part of it all…the first urge I have after seeing my score is to run and tell Deacon.

———

"I SAID A DRESS. NOT A NEW WARDROBE." I shake my head at the rack Heather pulls out for me.

"Shh. Who's the hot date? This is sudden."

"It's Deacon." I purse my lips and wait for her response.

"The asshole from work?" She hands me a black strappy dress. "This is the one." She hurries me into the dressing room but waves her hand forward like *continue*.

I close the door behind me and speak as I wiggle into the dress. "Yep. Same guy. I may have embellished on the asshole part."

"If you say so. I want details tomorrow over brunch."

"Deal. What happened with Stewart last night?"

"Girl, I don't know if you're ready. I'm sure you want to gloat but keep that shit to yourself if you value my discount."

That doesn't sound promising. "Oh no. What'd he do?"

"So, the apartment he's been taking me to isn't even his. He was watching it for a friend who was out of town. He finally came clean and took me to his real place last night."

I have to fight back a laugh. Not at her predicament, but at the fact there's no telling what's coming next.

"Oh, and the best part. I walked out of his room this morning and some older woman was standing there. She called me a whore and told me to put some clothes on. Yeah. It was his mom. He lives with her."

Wow. "Oh man, I'm sorry. Were you naked?"

"Yes!"

I step out of the changing room.

Her entire demeanor changes and her face lights up. "Oh, yeah. That's definitely the one."

I'm a little surprised she's not more upset about the Stewart situation, but the way she bounces around relationships, I guess she's just used to it. I do a little twirl in the mirror. "It's not too much?" I tug on the bottom, pulling it farther down my thighs. I'm afraid my ass will fall out the back, but it does look fantastic.

"Definitely the dress. I won't allow you to say no."

"Fine. So, what happened after his mom saw you naked?"

"The friend he was apartment sitting for was his ex-girlfriend."

"Shut up. You never noticed when you were there? How'd you find out?"

"After I got dressed and headed for the door, the ex showed up with a pair of my panties…"

"No. Way." I cover my mouth and shake my head.

"Yes. Way." She hangs her head, pretending to look sad. "I'm cursed."

I pull her in for a hug. "Maybe you need to try dating outside your usual type."

"What's my type?" She leans back.

"Pretty boys who look rich but might live with their mother."

"You have a valid point."

"You need a working man. Rough hands. Good heart. Humble."

"Too bad your dad isn't younger." She grins.

I smack her shoulder a little harder than intended. "You're terrible."

DEACON

COLD SWEAT BEADS across my forehead, and it hits me all at once. This shit with Quinn is real. She didn't turn me down.

I've never thought about my future with any woman, but it's all I think about with her. Taking her out on a few dates is the first step but what about everything to follow? Can I live up to that? Am I capable of giving her everything she deserves?

I gaze around my living room. It's manly and awesome. I like things the way they are—toys and gadgets and all my football shit.

What happens when she starts staying over and leaves stuff here?

I'm sure it'll start with a toothbrush or some clothes, maybe something to sleep in. She'll slowly take over my house like a virus until it's full of fruity candles and new curtains. Next thing I know she'll be asking to move in together and leaving wedding magazines on the counter. You know? Dropping subliminal hints like females do.

She'll replace my stuff with cozy little flower arrangements and throw pillows. Will she expect a ring on her finger soon? Will she pack up all my shit and reduce everything I was to nothing but a few boxes in the garage?

Will she start planning our family?

Yeah, she'll definitely do that. She'll use an app to show me what our kids will look like. She'll slowly erode my former life away piece by piece until I'm nothing but a shell of who I once was, floating around offshore, asking permission to buy season tickets to the Bears.

Get out of your head. You're freaking out for no reason.

I shrug, but surprisingly, that nightmare train of thought coursing through my brain doesn't bother me near as much as it should.

Being single has been fun. I can't lie about that. But I want Quinn. Besides, I'm sure we can take things slow. I know she says she's okay with the way things are, but I need to step up my game. She deserves the world, and if I can't give it to her, as hard as it would be, I need to let her move on.

A knock on my door sends me into a complete panic. I glance at my watch. It's nowhere near time to pick her up and I'm not expecting company.

"Open up, asshole." It's Dex.

I open the door. "The fuck you doing here?"

He breezes past me to the fridge and helps himself to a beer. "Need to plan Decker's bachelor party. I'm thinking big-titted strippers and booze." He waggles his brows and twists the top off a Bud Light.

It sounds like the exact opposite of what Decker would

want, but he's been acting like a dick, so it might be fun to watch his uncomfortable ass at a strip club.

"I have plans tonight."

He scoffs. "Plans? What's more important than embarrassing Decker for life?"

I look away and his twin intuition reads me like a book.

"Fucking hell. Remind me not to drink the water at the office. First Decker and now you?" Shaking his head, he takes a swig from the bottle. "Two little lovesick puppies." He points a finger at my face. "That's never happening to me. I need a cornucopia of pussy at my disposal at all times. Who's the lucky lady?"

I swallow, wondering if I should tell him. In the end, I can't keep it from him. He's my twin brother. We don't keep secrets.

Quinn agreed to the date. Surely, she doesn't mind if people find out since we're going to make things official. "Quinn."

Dexter's brows shoot up. "From the office?"

I nod.

"You okay? You look a little pale."

There's something about the way he stares at me. A wave of uncertainty crashes into my chest. Am I fooling myself to think a relationship with Quinn is possible? Judging by Dexter's face, he looks like I just suggested hell might freeze over.

I try to play it off and shrug. "Maybe I should cancel. What's up with the strippers?"

He takes a step back. "Damn, son. You're really twisted up inside."

It's impossible to hide shit from him. I nod, because it's true. I've never felt this way before.

"Look, man. I was just giving you shit. Don't cancel. Quinn's the best. Look how she puts up with all the shit we give her at work." He smirks, like everything makes more sense now. "You've been sending her those flowers and chocolates."

I nod again, waiting for him to call me a little bitch and rank my masculinity somewhere between 0 and 1.

"That chocolate was good, by the way. I stole some of it when she wasn't looking." He grins. "If you like her, fucking go for it, man." He takes a few steps toward the window and mumbles, "Quinn. Who woulda thought?"

"That's it? You're not gonna give me shit about this?"

"Oh, I will. Trust me. But I don't want to get blamed if you fuck it up." He grins. "Besides, you look like you're about to have a breakdown. You need to relax and enjoy the moment if this is your first date."

I'm not sure how to take all this. He's never acted this easygoing before. Something is up with him, but I realize he's right, and my confidence kicks back up to appropriate levels. "Thanks for the advice. You're a great American. Now stop drinking all my fucking beer and get out. I need to get ready and crush this like I do everything else in life. That means better than you."

He sets the beer down and walks to the door, then turns around at the last second. "Then stop being a pussy and live up to your name. You know what they say about the Collins brothers… Nobody fucks you harder, in the courtroom or the bedroom."

QUINN

I sweep my hair up for the millionth time and sigh. I can't decide if I should wear it in an updo or leave it down. I should've gotten ready at Heather's place. This is a disaster. I don't even know where I'm supposed to meet Deacon—or when.

What the hell? Why hasn't he called or texted?

I check my phone again for any messages. Nada. Nothing.

If he stands me up, I *will* kill him. I twist around, eyeing myself in the floor-length mirror on the back of my door. I glance at my phone for the millionth time but check the clock instead of my messages. Fortunately, I still have a few hours, and I need to make sure Dad gets fed before I leave. My mind races about this *date*.

What will happen after?

Will we go back to his place?

Calm down.

Should I take spare clothes?

No way. I don't want to look like I expect to spend the night.

Do I want to spend the night? If that's an option?

Pulling the dress off, I change into yoga pants and a t-shirt to make dinner. I don't want Dad burning the place down. Sometimes he forgets simple things, and I live in a constant state of anxiety. I'm worried he might be showing signs of early onset dementia. In my spare time I spend way too many hours staring at WebMD. I'm no doctor but the signs are present. I tell myself you can drive yourself crazy matching up symptoms on that site, but I'm worried this might be legit.

A few days ago, he was talking about Joe like they were going out for beer and wings like the old days. He played it off like he was reminiscing, but I saw the confusion etched on his face.

I walk into the living room just as he screams at some team on TV. It looks like hockey. Blackhawks maybe? It's difficult to keep up with all the different sports he watches.

My phone buzzes and my heart kicks into fifth gear, but it's a text from Heather wishing me luck tonight. I mentally curse her for a crime she doesn't know she committed.

Send me a damn text, Deacon! You're driving me insane.

Plating the old man's chicken and veggies, I realize he'll be eating alone tonight while I'm out having fun. Guilt creeps into my chest. I shouldn't feel this way, and he'd scold me if he knew about it. Outside our neighbors, nobody knows I take care of him except Heather and Tate, and I haven't told Tate much.

We don't ask for handouts and I don't need anyone thinking we're some charity case. Sure, we struggle to get by here and there, but our life is good. We have each other.

Sometimes Dad tells his doctors about our situation and I see the pity in their eyes. We don't need people feeling sorry for us. I don't take care of him out of obligation. It's because I love him and that's what you do.

He turns to me after I set his dinner on a TV tray. "I'm dining alone I see." His lips turn up into a smile. "Big plans?"

"I have a date."

I toss him a wink and walk to my room to avoid an interrogation. Okay, it's also to see if Deacon replied to my messages yet.

Zero notifications.

I frown but soldier on as planned. I decide to leave my hair down since I always wear it up at work. Once satisfied from the neck up, I wiggle into the form-fitting dress and slip on my shoes. They're wedge peep toes. Heather insisted they went perfect with the dress to show off my legs and add a few inches to my height.

When I walk back to the living room Dad whistles but says, "Where's the rest of your dress?"

I give him a stern look.

"Should probably get a coat on. I have my old trench—"

I cut him off. "Oh stop. It's not that revealing."

His cheeks redden and he lets out a snort of derision. "Who's the guy?"

"Someone from work."

He points at me with his good arm. "Better not lay a

hand on you. I mean it." His words come out as a growl, and I haven't seen him look this way in a while.

My heart warms and at the same time I glance down at his wheelchair. "Gonna run over his toes?"

He taps the armrest and grins. "I have a shotgun in the side of this thing that'll pop right out. Ronnie helped me install it."

I shake my head. "You're ridiculous." Secretly, I'm a bit worried he might not be lying.

"Whether I can walk or not, you'll always be my princess."

"I know, Dad." I bend down and plant a kiss on his forehead.

"Seriously though, you look beautiful. You make me proud, kiddo. I hope you know that. This guy better realize how lucky he is. Make sure he treats you right."

"Stop, Dad. You're gonna ruin my makeup."

"Okay, okay. But I mean every word."

"I still have the pepper spray you gave me." I wink.

On the inside, my stomach churns. Deacon still hasn't called or texted and it's only a few minutes before seven and I don't know where the hell I'm going. Surely, he didn't get cold feet. He seemed so determined when he asked me out.

The doorbell rings.

What. The. Hell.

I freeze and glare at Dad. "Plan on having Ronnie over without telling me?"

Dad shakes his head. "No. He's working tonight." He grunts and moves to unlock his chair.

"Stay put. I got it." It's probably one of the

neighborhood women he has wrapped around his finger. Who knows what they're going to do when I leave.

I open the door and my face pales.

Shit!

It's Deacon.

How the hell does he know where I live?

DEACON

THE DOOR SWINGS open and Quinn smiles for a brief second—then glares.

What'd she expect?

I told her I was doing this thing the right way. That means I pick her up at her house. She will *not* drive and meet me at our first date. I bribed Rick to find out where she lives and now I owe his ass another favor, but it's worth it. She needs to know I'm serious about dating her. Courting her? Is that what the fuck it's called? Regardless, it will be done correctly, and I will do it better than any other man on the planet.

"Hey."

She lowers her voice and whisper-screams. "What are you doing here?"

"It's not a real date unless I pick you up. That's how the world works." I lean in to kiss her cheek, but she dodges me and moves to block the doorway. She shuts the door behind her when I hear some guy yell in the background. I try to glance over her shoulder, but she gets it shut before I can see inside.

"You live with someone?"

She winces. "My dad."

I rub my chin and glance back to the door. "Are you ashamed of me?"

Her eyes widen. "What? No. It's just, you know?" She hems and haws for a brief second. "Meeting the parents isn't a first date thing, right?"

I brush my lips against hers but quickly stop myself and pull back. I don't want to come on too strong. "God, you look beautiful."

Her cheeks turn a slight shade of pink. "Thanks, you clean up pretty nice yourself." She shakes her head back and forth. "I was really worried there for a while. You could've called."

"I wanted to surprise you, and I knew you wouldn't let me pick you up."

"Yeah, you're right. That's exactly what would've happened."

I gesture toward her apartment. "I want to meet him." I twist the knob and push the door open.

Quinn stiffens. "No, Deacon…"

I'm already past her.

She follows behind, tugging at my bicep. "Just wait…"

"I'll take him out at the knees!" A gruff voice rings through the apartment as I turn the corner.

I stop immediately before I'm in his line of sight and turn to face her.

Quinn's lips curl up into an amused grin. She shrugs. "You wanted to meet him."

I take a deep breath. Fuck it. I want to impress him, and I want him to know his daughter is in safe hands.

I walk around the corner just as he's in the middle of barking another threat.

The moment his gaze meets mine he squints and then his eyes light up. "Deacon fucking Collins?"

I turn and smile just in time to catch Quinn rolling her eyes harder than I've ever seen.

This will be fun.

QUINN

I watch as Dad morphs from threatening to break Deacon's knees to shaking his hand and grinning like a boy on the playground. He's absolutely starstruck, and I have no idea why.

What the hell? Do they know each other?

"Quarterback for Illinois!"

"Yes, sir." Deacon nods.

Great.

Dad is the biggest football fan in the world. If they start chatting, I'll never get Deacon out of here. I leave them alone for a moment to grab Dad something to drink from the kitchen. When I return, he's gushing over a big play Deacon made in some bowl game.

It's simultaneously cute and annoying. I thought dads were supposed to revile the guys who dated their daughters.

"I still can't believe that injury. Man, the Bears were going to take you in the first round."

Deacon smiles like he's had this conversation a

thousand times, but doesn't show any signs of irritation. "It was a setback, but things turned out okay."

"Coulda used you out there on Sundays."

"I appreciate the kind words." Deacon looks up at me. "We should get going, but can I have just one minute with him?"

"Sure." I lean up against the wall.

They both stare at me like I'm some kind of disease, like I should know exactly what's going on.

"I meant in private." Deacon's eyes narrow on me.

I glance back and forth between them. "You're banishing me in my own apartment?"

Deacon gives me a look like he's already pleading for my forgiveness. "Please?"

I huff out a sigh and toss my hands up. "Fine." I walk through the hall toward the bedroom but stop where I can still hear their conversation.

"I just wanted to reassure you, sir. I will personally see to your daughter's safety this evening."

Before I can catch myself, my palm is on my chest and my face has to be bright pink. It might be the sweetest damn thing I've ever heard and has totally redeemed him for exiling me to the bedroom.

"Well, look. I like you, kid. And you were a damn good football player. She might look like a woman to you, but she's my little girl and she's my life. I am trusting you. So, I only have one piece of advice."

"Sir?"

"Don't fuck up."

"Yes, sir. She'll be treated with nothing but the respect she deserves."

"All right, then. You take care of her, or I'll take care of your other knee."

"Understood. I suppose I should go get her before she takes care of both of us."

"You catch on quick, son. I think you'll do just fine."

Shit!

I have to speed down the hall as fast as my shoes allow before Deacon catches me. My heart speeds up as he approaches the room. Finally, he opens the door.

I glance up at him and pretend to be irritated when I really want to jump up, wrap my legs around his waist, and kiss him until the sun comes up. "You guys done?"

He takes a step into the room and holds his hand out. "Sorry about that. No more distractions, promise. You ready?"

I take his hand and nod, unable to hold back my smile. "Okay." The second our hands touch, my heart races a million miles-an-hour and adrenaline floods my veins. I can't help but think this is the beginning of something new, something fresh and exciting. It all just feels—right, and I don't know if I've ever felt this way before.

I kiss Dad on the cheek on our way out. "Bye."

"You two have a good time." He gives Deacon a thumbs up.

Classic Dad move.

"Don't worry, sir. I'll have her home at a decent hour." Deacon flashes a mischievous grin my direction as he says it.

On our way to the car, I eye him up and down. He's wearing a suit that probably costs more than my car payment. You wouldn't know it by the way he carries himself, though. He's confident and cocky, but I've never seen him speak to anyone like he's better than them, even at the office with his subordinates.

Part of me worried he would see where I come from and give me the brush off. It's silly, I know, but I've dealt with so many rich clients and attorneys who treat me like I'm nothing more than the help. I don't come from his world of big money. I work hard for everything I have, but I know that trait isn't exclusive to poor people. I've noticed over the past few months there's more to Deacon than I realized.

I really like this side of him. In fact, I like it a lot.

"Where you taking me?"

Deacon walks around and opens my door. It's insanely cute at how attentive he's being to every single detail, to make sure he gets our first date right.

"It's a surprise."

"What if I don't like surprises?"

"Guess I better drop you back at your house and see if your dad wants to go to dinner." He winks.

"Such a comedian."

"If I didn't know better, I'd think you're jealous your old man likes me so much." Deacon pulls out of the apartment complex and hops on a highway.

"You caught me, sir. I'm green with envy." I laugh. "Really, though? That didn't go exactly the way I envisioned."

"So, you envisioned me meeting your dad?"

I smirk and glance at the trees and billboards flying by on the side of the road. "So cocky."

His hand goes to my thigh and engulfs my body in

flames. How does he do that? It's a normal gesture. He's not trying anything, but I can't help but notice how every single touch of his sends my body into the stratosphere.

"I enjoyed meeting him. He's a nice guy."

When we pull up to a hotel, my jaw clenches and I shoot Deacon a frown from hell.

He snickers, completely ignoring my reaction. "Oh, wipe that damn look off your face. It's not what you think. Trust me."

"I *do* trust you, Deacon."

That's what scares me.

He opens the door for me and we walk toward the hotel. I can tell Deacon's nervous but he hides it well. It's so cute.

His hand slips down to mine and our fingers interlace. We both look down at our hands at the same time, then back at each other and smile. Everything about this is perfect so far.

He leads me to a private elevator, and I never want him to let go of my hand. When we step out, it's the most beautiful rooftop garden I've ever seen—twinkling lights, flowers, candles, and fancy champagne—swallowed by lit up skyscrapers on all four sides, jutting into the night sky.

I know people always say things take their breath away, but the sight before me truly leaves me breathless.

I smile at Deacon. Everything else in my life—all my worries and fears and stress—fades away in this one moment, and I'm just a girl on a date with a guy who likes me. Deacon has outdone himself.

"Impressed?" He pulls my chair out for me.

"You could say that." I should tease him and make him

work a little harder for compliments, but I don't. I've never been on a date like this.

"You seem surprised." He takes a seat across from me and peels back the label from a cork on a bottle of champagne.

"I am. No one has ever done anything like this for me. I just don't understand. Why me?"

He pops the cork from the bottle and fills my glass. "I could sit here and list your good qualities all night long, but it's really pretty simple. I like you. You're worth the effort."

I take a sip and try to absorb everything and live in the moment. When he puts all the focus on me, it makes me a little uncomfortable. I'm not used to people heaping praise. Not that I want it or ask for it, but it *is* really nice. Everyone loves to hear someone appreciate them.

I need to change the subject, though. The spotlight has been on me long enough. "Had no idea you were *that* big of a football star."

He stares off at the surrounding buildings. "It's nothing."

"Don't be modest. My dad's a fanatic and straight shooter. If he didn't think you were any good, he'd have told you."

His gaze lands back on mine. "I was okay. Could have gone pro, but I blew out my knee." He shrugs. "It happens. Just glad I had my family and the firm to fall back on. What about you? I didn't know you lived with your dad."

If there's one thing I've noticed since Deacon showed up at my house, it's that he hasn't shown a hint of judgment for me living with my dad in our tiny apartment.

"It's not really something I broadcast to people. Dad was really independent. He drove a bus for the city for like twenty years. My mom dropped me off with him when I was five and I never saw her again. He raised me all by himself. A few years back, he had a stroke and suffered severe nerve damage. Couldn't work anymore. So, it was my time to take care of him."

"But why don't you tell anyone? Maybe people would help out or whatever? He seems like a social guy. I'm sure he's made a lot of friends in his life."

I shake my head. "It's my job, and I don't want anyone feeling sorry for us. When your family needs you, you stick together. I don't know if I'd trust anyone else, anyway."

Deacon gives me a look, like he senses not to press harder. "Well, he seems like a great guy."

I smile.

"I'm sure he has to be."

"Why?"

"He raised a remarkable daughter."

"He's the best..." I shake my head and a million feelings sock me in the chest all at once. *Not now. Not here.* The past plays through my mind, of how Dad was before, and now after.

Deacon takes my hand in his from across the table. "You know you can talk to me. I'm not just saying that to be nice. I *want* to know you and your family."

I let out a breathy exhale. "I'm worried he's showing signs of early onset dementia."

Deacon leans in. "What kind of signs?"

"Little things, like mood swings, short-term memory

loss, some days he can almost take care of himself and some days he's almost helpless." I wipe at the corner of my eye.

"Hey, hey, it's fine." His hand covers mine. "Maybe we should talk about something else on our first date. Save the heavy tears for date two." Deacon grins.

I laugh and nod. "Please. That would be great."

"I want to know everything, but you look so beautiful and it's so nice out here. I didn't mean to dig all that up right out the gate." He leans back in his chair and folds his hands behind his head. "Ask anything about me. I'm an open book."

"Favorite movie?"

"*Die Hard*. Next."

I snicker.

"What? Who doesn't love *Die Hard*? It's the greatest Christmas movie of all time."

"Uhh, it's *so* not a Christmas movie."

Deacon's eyebrows shoot up. "It *so* is. Not even just a Christmas movie, the greatest, like I said. Next."

I can't stop laughing then I stop and just look into his eyes and smile.

"What is it?"

"Nothing, you just… you'll get along great with Dad."

"I should hope so. He has excellent taste in cinema and quarterbacks."

How did he take me from the brink of tears to smiling and laughing like a fool within ten seconds?

We drink, eat, and laugh.

The night goes by far too fast and before I know it, he's walking me to my door. I don't know why I feel so nervous right now. Our first date is perfect, and I never want it to end. It's light years beyond any other date I've ever been on, like something from a movie or a book.

"I really enjoyed tonight." His lips brush up against mine as he backs me up against the door. It's not a normal kiss from him, but it still knocks the breath out of me. His mouth moves slowly over mine. No tongue.

My knees go weak at how sensual it is. It's a gentle and dominant kiss at the same time. A kiss that says *you're mine*. It's a kiss that says he cares about me, wants more than just sex in a closet.

Whatever he's doing, it's working because I already feel the familiar throb between my legs, and tingles skittering over my skin.

I'm ready for it. I want him so damn bad right now, and it's not just to get off. I want to feel the connection between us. Something tells me sex with him right now would be on an entirely different plane of existence. Mentally, I'm begging his thick frame to crash into me, pin me up against something.

He pulls back, and I let out a sigh before I can stop it. I can't tell if I'm annoyed or dazed or both, but I instantly miss him pressed up against me.

I gesture toward the apartment. "You know…he's asleep. I could show you my room. You didn't get to see it before."

Deacon lets out a slight groan. "God, don't do this to me right now." His hand shoots out in front of me, palm up. "Sorry, that came out wrong."

I stand there and stare, unable to form words.

Is he really about to turn down sex again? What world am I living in?

Deacon reaches up and tugs at his hair.

He looks so freaking hot in his suit, warring with himself to the point he might pull his hair out. Flames roar through my body and lick down to my fingers and toes at the sight of this gorgeous man who wants me so bad he has to fight it. I want to jump up and wrap my legs around him, refuse to let go until he comes inside.

"I can't believe these words are about to leave my lips, but no."

My eyes widen. "No?"

He places both palms on my cheeks and plants another soft kiss on my lips and I'm not sure how much more I can take.

When he leans back, his eyes plead with me. "Please. All I want is the perfect ending to tonight. I want to watch you go through that door, and I want to miss you like crazy the second it shuts. Then, I want to walk to my car, drive home, and replay the moment over and over in my head until it's seared into my brain. The perfect moment from our perfect first date, so I can tell the story fifty years from now and remember every single vivid detail. The way a first date should be." He reaches out and pulls me in close to him. His hands slide down my dress and cup my rear. "But, so you don't think I've turned into a total pussy, I *will* collect on this offer in the future." He kisses my neck. "Again." He squeezes my ass. "And again." Deacon kisses me once more, hard enough to bruise my lips, and I can tell he's fighting everything in his body to not haul me into the apartment and do unspeakable things.

Holy mother.

When we separate, I give him exactly what he asked for. I turn back and flash him one last smile and an awkward wave before I close the door.

What he doesn't know, is I'm doing the exact same thing he is right now. Taking in the moment, so I can remember it clear as day in the future. It's almost impossible to focus because he looks so damn—just happy, like a young boy after he just gave a girl a flower for the first time. I have to be grinning like a damn idiot. The night was perfect. Absolutely perfect.

Once I close the door, I turn and my back hammers against it and I gasp for air. I press the pad of my fingertips to my swollen lips and whisper, "Wow."

DEACON

QUINN HAS no idea how difficult it was to not throw her over my shoulder and haul her to her bedroom.

I think my dick is still pissed at me about it.

I wanted to so damn bad, but I just couldn't. I promised myself I would do this thing right and treat her with the respect she deserves. I really liked her dad too, and I made a promise to him. There's no way in hell I was going to go into their apartment and fuck her while he was asleep in the next room.

Even though Quinn said it was fine, I would never disrespect him like that. Not going to happen. Her dad was a pleasant surprise. I didn't think it was possible, but now, I admire her even more; the way she takes care of him, goes to law school, and works a full-time job.

She is a total badass and I feel like the ultimate slacker.

I can see now why she was so averse to dating someone, especially me. Look at everything she has going on in her life.

I'm going to have to do better if I want to stay in a relationship with her.

A relationship.

I'm in one now, and it feels awkward and awesome at the same time. I don't think I've ever really been serious with another woman. Sure, I've "dated" or whatever, but it was just hooking up more than once. It's never felt real, until Quinn.

When I pull up the driveway, I can't shake the excitement. I'm practically bouncing on the balls of my feet, ready to hit somebody. It's better than walking through the tunnel at the Rose Bowl in Pasadena or after winning the Big Ten championship my senior year. And that shit was insane. I never thought I'd feel an adrenaline rush like it again.

After a long shower, I crawl into bed and try to watch something on TV. Nothing holds my interest. I must flip through the channels for like forty-five minutes.

I keep glancing over and staring at my phone. I feel like such a pussy because I want to call a friend and tell them all about my date. Dex is about the only one that'd understand, but I still don't know if he'd *get* it. Really, there's only one person I want to talk to right now.

Fuck it. I'm calling her.

Quinn answers on a yawn after the third ring. "Deacon?"

"Shit, did I wake you up?"

"No. It's fine. I was just getting into bed."

"You don't have to lie. You go to bed early as fuck, don't you?"

"10:42 p.m."

"Huh?"

"Nothing, I was just seeing how long you could go without using profanity. I know you were doing it for our date."

I look at my clock on the nightstand and it's 10:42. I can't do anything but smile and plead ignorance. "I was?"

"Okay, I'll be honest if you will. I was asleep. But it's okay. It's nice to hear your voice."

"Okay, well, when I got home I shouted 'fuck' roughly forty-eight times to make up for any f-bombs I would've normally dropped between the hours of seven and nine."

A laugh comes through the receiver. I've never made her laugh this much in the past. She's warming up to me, a lot.

"Okay, I'm up. What's going on?"

I contemplate making something up, but I just told her we were being honest. "I just promised not to lie, so here it goes. I need to say something, and I don't really have anyone else I can talk to about it. Nobody who won't give me shit, anyway."

"What's up?"

"Well, you're pretty much my best friend, outside of my brothers, and I..."

"Spit it out, Collins."

"Okay. Well, I had an amazing first date with the perfect girl tonight, and I just wanted to tell someone."

She sniffles.

"Fuck, are you crying?"

"No! Don't be ridiculous." She sniffles again. "No... it's just, allergies. And God, you can be really sweet when you want to be. Do you know that?"

"I'm like that candy that's really sour at first then sweet when you get to the middle."

She laughs. "Yes! Perfect analogy. And Deacon..."

"Yeah?"

"I had a really great time too."

"You did?"

"Yeah, see there's this guy...I never really knew what to make of him. We've been sleeping together for months, but I never took him seriously until now."

"Well, he sounds amazing. You should see him again."

"You really think I should? I'm kinda into him."

"Absolutely, I bet his dick is huge."

Quinn bursts into a laugh. "I don't know about the last part. He's pretty average. But maybe I will. He knows how to use his tongue, after all."

I can't stop grinning. "Hey, Quinn?"

"Yeah?"

"Thanks for listening. Goodnight."

"Goodnight, Deacon."

I end the call and feel like I might float up to the ceiling.

Fuck, life is good.

QUINN

I UNROLL my yoga mat next to Heather's.

She nudges me with her elbow. "So, how was it?" She bends down and slips off her shoes.

I take a quick sip from my water bottle before class starts. "Perfect."

"Oh wow, look at you, cheesing like a fool. Must've been damn good." She waggles her eyebrows.

I shake my head at her. "Wasn't like that. He reserved a private rooftop. We had dinner and champagne. The conversation was amazing, then he drove me home and kissed me goodnight."

She stops unrolling her mat and stares at me. "That's it? No foreplay? You *have* already banged this guy, right?"

"I'm serious." I swat at her. "It was nice, perfect even. He called me when he got home because he couldn't stop thinking about me."

"He gonna come over tonight to wash and braid your hair too?" She cackles but clears her throat when the instructor shows up.

167

I scowl at her and face forward.

"Good morning, class."

"Good morning," everyone says in unison.

"Let's get into position. We'll start with upward facing dog."

"Should be a first for you." Heather makes sure to say it when the instructor isn't watching and shoots out her tongue.

I pretend to scratch my nose and use my middle finger.

After turning my attention back to yoga, I focus on my breathing and relax. I stick to the beginner's class since I rarely have time to come, and feel like a newbie every time.

"Chin up, Quinn," the instructor says.

I do as she says and my muscles strain in the best way possible.

"Hold your position. Good. Now let's get in to downward dog."

The next thirty minutes fly by without Heather yapping in my ear. She's my best friend and I love her dearly, but it's nice to keep some of my feelings about Deacon private. I like having him all to myself.

Heather leaves to get ready for work. They're doing the monthly inventory tonight, but I'm not ready to go home yet. I don't get many free evenings. After I change, I head off down the street with my gym bag.

I duck inside one of my favorite coffee shops and splurge on a white mocha latte with a dash of cinnamon. I pay and grab my drink, then walk through the small park on the way to the apartment, watching the kids play. They're so carefree, without a worry in the world. No crazy course schedule or workload. No bills. No sick parent to take care of.

It's nice to watch them, and I find myself wondering when I went from *that* to my current state. It didn't happen overnight. Adulthood doesn't smack you in the face, it creeps up on you slowly until one day you no longer recognize yourself.

I scroll through my phone and think about sending Deacon a text, but I remember he has Decker's bachelor party today. Wow, finally a free night and Deacon's busy. I could never ask him to skip the party, though. That would be ridiculous and irrational and something I'd never do. But, I can secretly wish he was here, spending time with me. Nothing wrong with that.

Tate flew to Dallas for the weekend to hang out with her friends back home for her bachelorette party. She invited me to go but there was no way I could leave Dad. Who am I kidding? I couldn't afford the flight, even if I'd wanted to go. It was sweet of her to offer, though.

Before I realize, it gets late and I need to head home and make dinner. I try to stick to a routine with Dad as much as I can. As I walk up the sidewalk toward our building, I freeze in my tracks. There's an ambulance out front, and blue and red lights swirl and reflect off the buildings. EMTs wheel someone out the door on a gurney. My coffee hits the sidewalk and explodes into the air. I take off in a dead sprint.

Please, don't let it be him. Please, don't let it be him.

It's him.

Olly, the landlord, meets me at the ambulance. "He had

a fall and bumped his head. Ronnie heard him yell for help. He's going to be okay, Quinn. Don't worry."

My head spins so fast I feel dizzy. It's too much to take in all at once. He'll be okay. He *has* to be.

They won't let me in the ambulance with him. There's no room and they're trying to hurry in case he had another stroke.

The EMT guy shouts, "University of Chicago Medical Center."

I rush to my car so I can follow.

DEACON

DECKER ROLLS his eyes and knocks back another shot at the strip club. "You assholes plan this for me or yourselves?" He lets out a derisive snort.

I hold both hands up. "Don't look at me. This was the other two." I point a finger and wave it between Dexter and Donavan. All I want is to hang out with Quinn right now, but I'm stuck here. There's no way I could get out of it and time is dragging ass.

A brunette with giant fake tits takes to the pole. Her ass cheeks clap against a dental-floss thong as our idiot brothers throw wads of dollar bills at her. They both have unlit cigars hanging from their mouths and laugh it up. I can't help but think only a few months ago I'd have been right there with them. That was the old Deacon, though.

Part of me smiles at the sight. At least Decker and Donavan are in the same room together. Shit has been tense between them ever since Donavan called Weston and told him about Tecker. They need to kiss and make up.

I've never seen my brothers pissed at each other for longer than a day or two.

"I'd have been happy with a night of poker." Decker downs another drink. "Fuck, imagine all the germs in this shit hole."

I nod. "I hear you."

Decker rolls his eyes. I know he doesn't believe me, but he doesn't know about Quinn and me. I haven't told anyone but Dex. I don't want to make shit weird for her at work and Dex won't say anything. There's no way she'd be fired. I'd make sure of that, but she doesn't need the added anxiety. She has enough to worry about as it is.

"You seeing this shit?" Dex howls and points at the stage. The stripper is picking up dollar bills with the ol' downstairs.

"Fuck." I look away.

This is not my damn scene at all. In fact, it's a little repulsive. I can't believe I used to enjoy this kind of shit.

I would rather be anywhere in the world but here. What I'd love most, is to take Quinn to dinner, or just hang out and watch a movie.

I know I sound like a pussy, but I don't give a single fuck. I wonder if Decker would kill me if I left early? I glance at my phone to see if Quinn has texted.

"What's with you? You seem distracted. Somewhere else you'd rather be?"

"Who me?"

"Yeah, you, dipshit. What's her name?"

"Who?"

"Whoever's call you're expecting on your phone. You can't stop staring at it."

Before I can answer, my phone rings and Quinn's name flashes on the screen.

"Don't think I don't know it was you who messed with all the shit in my…"

His words trail off and everything else fades away when I swipe the screen. "Gotta take this." I cover the receiver until I'm outside. "Hey."

"Deacon." My name filters through the speaker on a sob.

My hand grips the phone so tight my knuckles turn white and my stomach twists. "What's wrong?"

"It's my dad… he umm, fell. I'm on my way to the hospital and I didn't know who else to call. I couldn't ride with him. They wouldn't let—"

"What hospital? I'm on my way."

"No, you have Decker's thing. I'm being selfish. I just wanted to hear your voice for a second."

She sounds like she's about to have a breakdown and all I want to do is hold her in my arms.

"Decker will understand. What hospital?"

"University of Chicago Medical Center."

"Everything will be fine. He'll be okay. Just drive safe, I'm on my way." I take off in a dead sprint for the street. The only thing that matters right now is how fast I can get to her. I hail a cab and must scare the shit out of the cabbie when I leap in.

"University of Chicago Medical Center! Now!" I pull three hundred bucks from my wallet and toss it up in his seat. "As fast as you can."

I ARRIVE at the hospital and see Quinn alone in the waiting area. I rush up to the desk before she can cut me off.

"Why the hell isn't she back there with her dad?"

The lady behind the counter holds her hands up and her eyes turn into two huge white orbs.

I point back at Quinn, but don't even turn. "This shit is unacceptable. I want her back there. *Now!*"

Quinn puts her hand on my arm and turns me to face her. "It's okay. I saw him already." She bolts into my arms. I yank her close to me and run my hand up and down her back, then hold the back of her head in my palm and smooth her hair with it. I should feel terrible about her father, but at the same time I can't help but think this is what I'm meant to do. Be there for her when she needs me. Everything in my world feels right again.

I pull back from her, place both palms on her cheeks, and swipe her tears away with my thumbs. "What happened?"

"God, I don't know, just...thank you for coming. I would've called Heather but she's working and I..."

"Just, slow down. It's going to be fine. I'm glad you called."

Her bloodshot eyes meet mine. "You are?"

"Of course I am. So what's going on?"

"I wasn't home. I was walking through the park and saw the ambulance and it all happened so fast. They took me back to see him right when we got here, but now they're doing some kind of scan and making sure he didn't have another stroke. I guess he tried to change chairs but forgot to lock his wheels in place. He hit his head on the corner of the entertainment stand."

I breathe a sigh of relief. Sounds like a bump on the head, but I make sure not to downplay anything. "I'm sure everything will be fine. He's tough as nails."

Quinn shakes her head. "I should've been there."

"It's not your fault. Accidents happen."

"I know, but still. He's my responsibility. If I'd been there…"

"You can't hover over him twenty-four seven. You could've been in the shower or the kitchen. He won't blame you." I kiss her temple and hold her against me.

The nurse comes through the double doors and calls Quinn over.

I follow.

"He didn't have another stroke but we're going to keep him overnight to monitor for signs of a concussion. Sorry, I know you were worried out here. You can go back in and see him now."

I shoo Quinn away when she glances back at me. "Go. I'll wait out here."

She follows the nurse.

I walk over to the desk. The woman looks like she might have a panic attack with me standing there.

"I'm very sorry. I didn't know she'd already been back to see him."

The woman nods. "It's okay. No problem."

"No, it's not okay. I should've had all the facts before I started in on you. I apologize."

"Okay, well, apology accepted, sir."

"Thank you." I step outside for some fresh air and text Decker.

Deacon: Sorry. Had to bounce. Something important came up.

Decker: Something or someone?

Deacon: Both.

Decker: Everything okay?

Deacon: It will be, but I can't make it back out. I'm sorry.

Decker: It's fine. You owe me.

WHEN QUINN finally returns from the room, she's smiling. "Thanks for coming and waiting. Sorry if I was a little dramatic on the phone."

He must be doing okay if she's smiling.

"Don't mention it. Is he okay?"

"I think so. He's a little shaken up, but everything is normal."

"Good. So, you heading out?"

"Yeah. For a bit. Dad said we both need rest and he'd have them throw me out if I didn't go get some sleep."

"I'll drive you home."

Quinn shakes her head. "That's not—"

"Quinn, I'm driving."

She nods and hands over the keys. We walk out through the ER and into the parking lot to her car. I open the passenger door for her, then walk around and climb in the driver's side.

The whole ride home I don't say much. I know she has a lot on her mind.

When we arrive, I walk her to the door. I give her a

kiss, but I don't want her to think I want more, with everything going on.

When our lips part ways, her eyes roam up to mine. "Stay with me? Please."

I know I told her we needed to take this slow, but fuck she's making it a torturous journey.

How the hell can I tell her no? It's impossible. There's nothing I want more than to hold her and comfort her—take care of her and make sure she has everything she needs. I give her a nod.

We both walk inside, and she heads to her bedroom. "Make yourself comfortable. I'm gonna change clothes."

"Sure." I pretend like I'm about to sit down, but once she's in her room I walk to the bathroom and start a bath for her. I find some lavender bath salts under the sink and dump them in. Once that's started, I pull out my phone to order a pizza. When that's done, I start back for the living room, but she appears in front of the bedroom door.

"Thought you were making yourself comfortable on the couch?"

I move out of her way and point to the tub. "Get in there. I don't want to hear from you for thirty minutes. I'll let you know when the food gets here.

"What kind of food?"

"Pizza."

She shakes her head. "I don't know how, but it seems like you can read my mind sometimes."

"I pay attention."

"Oh yeah? What kind of pizza did you get?"

"Mushroom and extra cheese." I walk past her and give

her a playful little slap on the ass, coupled with a wink. "You're welcome."

"Glad to see you're still as cocky as ever." The way she smiles as she says the words tells me I'm knocking it out of the park right now.

"Thirty minutes. No sooner. Relax. I'll hold down the fort."

———

FORTY-FIVE MINUTES LATER, she comes out of the bathroom wearing silly pajama pants with rubber ducks on them and a matching tank top. I can see her nipples through the thin material and my cock takes notice.

I tug on her pantleg as she sits down on the couch. "Nice pants."

"Wore them just for you." Quinn curls into me and it feels so fucking good to just hold her. "Thank you for the bath. It was perfect. You always know just what I need."

A movie plays in the background on the TV but I can't stop staring at her.

She wiggles her ass against me to get comfortable and it's a little bit of heaven and hell at the same time. "I'm glad you're here. Thank you."

I push a few strands of hair behind her ear. "Nowhere I'd rather be." I tilt her chin up and kiss her softly on the lips. This is fucking perfect.

The door buzzes. It must be the pizza.

Quinn starts to get up.

I stop her. "I got it. Just lie there and relax."

"Yes, sir." She grins.

Fuck, even the way she calls me "sir" makes my dick hard.

I walk back with the pizza and set it on the coffee table. "I still don't know what kind of normal human being from Chicago doesn't like deep dish."

Quinn shrugs. "Can't help what I like." She takes a piece straight out of the box like *fuck plates*. "And I can't believe you remembered my favorite place, and the exact pizza I always order."

"I've seen you haul in leftovers to the office. I notice everything about you."

Quinn takes a huge bite and her eyes roll back like she's in heaven. "I can't argue with you. You're batting one hundred."

I laugh. "That's actually a baseball stat, and one hundred is piss poor. One thousand is perfect."

She shrugs, not even remotely interested in anything but her pizza. "Well, I gave it my all."

"I applaud your effort."

QUINN

IT'S UNDERSTATING things to say I'm nervous about leaving Dad on his own today, but he did fine the last few days when I finally went back to work. I really didn't need to take two days off last week, but Deacon went over my head to Decker and insisted they give me the time. It's been one week since the fall.

I'm still surprised Deacon didn't try anything while we were alone at the house. All he did was hover over me and rush to get anything I needed. It was sweet and cute and so not how I imagined him handling any kind of crisis.

Nerves flutter through my stomach thinking about him. I'm heading to his apartment; we still haven't had sex since we started dating. It's been nice getting to know him, but I'd be lying if I said I didn't miss the sex. A girl has needs. I'm afraid it'll be different, now that there's an emotional connection there. Still, if there's one thing I do know, it's that I want sex. I want sex with Deacon, bad.

When I arrive at his apartment, he greets me with a kiss. "I'm almost ready."

"Okay." I grin at the walls. It seriously looks like he hired my dad to decorate.

"That helmet's signed by Tom Brady."

"Who?" I smile. It's fun messing with him. Even I know who Tom Brady is.

"You're joking right?"

I laugh. "Yeah. He's married to Gisele."

Deacon shoots me a playful glare. "That the only reason you know who he is?"

I shrug. "Is there anything else important about him?"

He strolls over and takes my hands in his. "Did you know you're perfect?"

"I am? What am I doing here with you then?" I smirk.

He hooks an arm around my waist and tickles my ribs. Our lips meet and going out to lunch just became an afterthought.

"Fuck, I've missed your smart-ass mouth. Nice to have you back."

"That all you missed?" I whisper.

"No. I missed these too." His lips pepper sweet kisses down my throat as his hands slide down to my breasts over my t-shirt.

Finally!

Deacon wastes no time gripping the hem of my shirt and pulling it over my head. A groan strains from his throat when he gets a full look at the white sheer lace bra I'm wearing.

"These. Off." He fumbles with the button of my jeans, and I kick off the red leather heels I wore just for him. The moment my jeans are off, Deacon lifts me to his chest.

My legs hook around his waist, and he carries me to his bedroom.

"Your clothes are in my way now, Mr. Collins."

"We should do something about that."

"Yes, we should."

"Someone wants to get laid."

I shake my head and kiss him again. "You have no idea."

"Well, well, my dirty little office slut is still in there."

Any other man would get kneed in the balls for talking to me like that, but right now, in the moment, it's hot as all hell. Excitement swirls down and pools between my thighs at his filthy mouth. He heaves me onto the bed, and I realize something. Not only is this my first time in *his* bed, but it's our first time in a bed at all.

It feels like we should celebrate or something. I suppose the sex will be enough of a reward, but there's something special about the moment.

I'm not sure how, but his clothes are off in an instant, as if they've magically disappeared.

He hovers over me and brushes a lock of hair behind my ear. "You have no idea how many times I've imagined this." His strong hands roam my body as he looms above, staring into my eyes. "Alone. In my room. No time constraints."

I gulp at the look in his eyes right now. He looks one part wolf, one part lion.

He traces a finger along the curve of my shoulder. "Do you have any idea how beautiful you are?"

"I enjoy hearing you tell me."

"Most beautiful woman I've ever seen." His lips land on mine.

It's soft and slow at first, but I need more than that. "Thank you, Mr. Collins." I bat my eyelashes at him, reach between his legs, and stroke his cock. It grows harder against my palm.

"Fuck, I'm going to enjoy this."

"I sure hope so, big guy." I smirk but all silliness leaves my face when those stormy eyes narrow on me.

His hand slides between my thighs. "Plenty big, but you already know that." His voice is coarse and laced with raw need. It's primal and makes my blood hum with desire.

My back arches into him, eager for his touch, longing for any kind of friction I can get.

Sliding down my body, his mouth replaces his hand between my legs. His nose presses against my panties and he breathes me in. "I like these. Too bad they're in my way." Deacon snaps the waistband in one possessive movement.

I let out a gasp before I can stop myself.

If I thought he was sexy and dominating in the supply closet...he's a whole other level of alpha in his bedroom. The look in his eyes tells me everything he wants to do to me, and I'd be lying if I said my heart rate doesn't redline at the sight of him.

I glance around the room. There's nothing personal on display other than a black and white photograph of him and his brothers. I almost ask him to turn it around. It's like their eyes are watching—judging—and waiting to score his performance.

If I say it he might think I'm crazy, but right now, I might just be crazy the way he's teasing me.

Slow and methodical, he kisses the tops of my thighs, taking his sweet-ass time. I need more of him, now, but he knows exactly what I want and withholds like he always does, teasing me into a frenzy. He bites down on my skin hard enough to leave a mark.

I let out a small yelp of approval and rake my nails through his hair.

Looking up at me he says, "This is mine." He flicks his tongue across my clit, his eyes fixed on me, watching every reaction. "Only mine, Quinn."

His words turn my insides to Jell-O. When he says things like that all my thoughts and reservations drift away. All I can do is nod in surrender.

"Fingers or mouth?" He teases at my clit with his tongue and slides a finger inside me.

I nod furiously.

"Use your words, Quinn." He slips the finger out, and I clench around nothing the second it leaves me.

My hips lift instinctively, practically begging for his touch, and all the breath steals from my lungs. "Both." It's the only word I can manage.

"So fucking greedy." His mouth latches onto my clit and the man is relentless. This time he pushes two fingers in deep and with more force.

Right when I'm on the edge of an epic orgasm, he lifts up, not letting me finish. "There's nothing better than watching you get off." He presses his mouth against my inner thigh and brushes his hands over my nipples. With one swift motion, he reaches up with both hands and jerks the cups of my bra down, leaving me exposed. His fingers grow possessive and dig into my hips as he yanks me against his face, over and over. "I could fuck this pussy with my mouth all goddamn day."

"I. No. Complain." The man turns my words to gibberish, and a light moan parts my lips.

He slides up my body, slanting over me.

His lips meet mine and against my mouth he whispers, "Can you taste yourself on my tongue?"

Oh. My. God.

Can he get any dirtier?

Yes. Yes he can. It's a ridiculous question.

Rocking back on his calves he pulls a condom from the nightstand drawer.

Pre-come beads on the head of his cock and I want to lick it off.

Deacon takes his time rolling the condom on. I watch the whole time, praying for him to hurry up and get me off. I'm practically writhing on his bed. If he so much as breathes on me I'll combust immediately.

There's something between us and we both feel it. I need to just give in and embrace it, put all my chips on the table, because not being serious with Deacon doesn't seem like an option.

He lies back and fists his dick so that it's pointed up at the ceiling.

I crawl toward him, unable to resist the pull vibrating through every atom of my body. I lift one leg and slowly slide down on him, until I've taken every last inch.

He groans as I squeeze around him, and his eyes roll

back for a brief second. "I've been dying for this. To have you in my bed, on top of me."

"Well, you have me." Our bodies move together in perfect rhythm, like we've done this a million times. In a way, it feels like we have. Right now, we're two old souls who've always shared a connection. I grind my hips in small circles, loving what it does to him.

His thumb goes straight to my clit, stroking back and forth across it while he watches my face. His other palm smacks my ass and he groans. "Fuck. Right there."

I shudder at his words, his thumb, his cock—all of him. As much as I love the way I feel when he's inside me, I also love knowing how crazy I drive him. That I can satisfy him as much as he satisfies me.

"That's it. Come on my dick. I want to feel you."

"Oh God, Deacon." My orgasm crashes through me, spinning and whirling like a hurricane.

His thumb speeds up on my clit and I ride the undulating waves until I'm breathless. I don't know how I manage not to collapse onto him. I'm running on pure determination and willpower right now.

"So. Close. Too." His eyes stay locked on mine the entire time, watching me come undone on top of him.

He finally places both hands on my hips and presses me down, so I take every bit of him as deep as possible. At the same time he grunts. His cock twitches inside me.

"Fuck, Quinn."

My eyes flutter open at the sight of him emptying himself, and for a brief second I wish he wasn't wearing the condom. I want to feel him bare inside me, filling me.

I shouldn't think that. It would be incredibly reckless

and stupid, but I can't help myself. I want to know what it'd feel like, what it'd be like. It should scare the hell out of me, but it doesn't. I can't form rational thoughts right now. My brain is a jumbled mess of exposed wires.

When he finishes, I collapse on top of him, and he holds me to his chest for what seems like an eternity, but probably isn't more than a few seconds. Then, I remember he's still inside me with a full condom and I roll off to his side.

We both lie there, panting, staring up at the ceiling. At the same time, we both turn over to face each other.

Through several labored breaths I say, "That was…"

"Incredible." He finishes the sentence for me.

I never want to get up. Never want to leave his bed again.

Eventually, my brain resumes its regular function, and I excuse myself to the bathroom.

Staring in the mirror, I splash cold water on my face.

Glancing around, I still can't believe I'm here with Deacon in his apartment. It's surreal after months of hooking up at work. Three months ago, if someone had told me I'd be dating one of the Collins brothers, I'd have died laughing. I'd have written them off as a crazy person.

But, here I am.

When I return to the room, Deacon's in front of his dresser pulling some clothes out. He tosses me an oversized t-shirt as he walks toward me. He stops and plants a kiss on my forehead, then shoulders past into the bathroom.

I have to stop and ogle him as he walks away. He's so —perfect, and male, and manly as all hell. His broad shoulders and thigh muscles expand and contract with each step. The way he walks almost looks like he's strutting, but it's not because he's some douche trying to look tough. It's because his chest is so damn wide it forces his arms out at an angle. I can't help myself and glance down from his back to between his legs. His thick cock hangs down, bouncing from side to side.

I can't help but give him a little catcall whistle.

"Enjoying the view?" he calls over his shoulder.

I bite my lower lip between my front teeth. "I am actually."

"Gonna end up in HR for sexual harassment." He closes the door to the bathroom, laughing on his way in.

"Worth it," I whisper to myself.

My body already starts to thrum with desire once more, just picturing him walking away from me. I pull his shirt over my head loving how it smells exactly like him.

He exits the bathroom still fully naked.

My cheeks pink at the sight of him from the front.

We just had sex in his bed.

"I love it when you blush." He walks up and traces my jaw with his finger. "Hungry?"

"Starving."

"Well then, how do you like your eggs?"

I smack at his chest, then grab it a little because it's hard as granite and I can't help myself. "Shut up. You cook?"

"I can do lots of things." He slips on his boxer briefs.

I follow him to the kitchen. "What can I do to help?"

He points at a bar stool along the kitchen island. "Just

sit your hot little ass there and look pretty. I got this." He kisses my nose.

"Okay then, hotshot. Let's see what ya got." I cringe at my awkward, accidental rhyme, and take a seat on the stool.

"Okay, Funkmaster Flex." He laughs. "I see you're sitting in the front row. Big shocker. Might wanna grab your notebook and pencil."

"So I can write a Yelp review trashing your eggs?"

"You're gonna regret that in a few minutes. Just wait." He pulls down a spatula from a hanging pot rack and points it at me. "You'll see."

I laugh and watch him go to work. God what a view. There's something inherently sexy about a man cooking in nothing but boxer briefs. His muscles expand and constrict at the slightest movements as he strolls around the kitchen. I swear he looks like a breathing Michelangelo sculpture.

He grins at me as he pulls bacon and eggs from the refrigerator. "Like omelets?"

"Yeah." Anything with Deacon sounds good. Why does it feel like all the air leaves the room when he's around? He makes me insane.

I can't believe he's cooking in his kitchen for me. It feels like a dream. This whole day has been amazing so far. I never want it to end, but I know as the sun inches down on the horizon, reality awaits. At some point, I'll need to go home and take care of Dad. I don't mind *that*. I just wish there was some way I could have everything I want all at once. My life seems like a zero-sum game. If I want time with Deacon, it has to come out of time with

Dad. And if I want time with Dad, it has to come out of time with Deacon.

I allow myself to briefly think about what it'd be like if we all lived together. It's insane, I know. But I wouldn't have to feel so torn between the two of them. Trying to be two places at once is exhausting. I'm allowed to think about what it'd be like, even if it would never happen.

"What's going on in that brain of yours?" He must notice the far-off look in my eyes.

"Wondering how terrible this omelet will be." I laugh and breathe a sigh of relief when he chuckles at my terrible joke.

There's no way in hell I'll tell him I was fantasizing about him living with Dad and me. It's so hilarious I almost laugh out loud but catch myself. I have this vivid picture of his reaction in my mind. It consists of his silhouette sprinting over the horizon, growing tiny in the sunset. He's in nothing but his boxer briefs, and he doesn't look back. Nope. Not once. There's nothing but a trail of dust kicked up in his wake.

I don't want to scare him off, but my feelings for Deacon are so intense. He makes me so happy. Happier than I've ever been.

"My lady." He does some medieval curtsy and slides a plate in front of me, then retrieves a glass of orange juice.

It looks so damn good I almost want to take a picture of it with my phone. I take a bite of the fluffy eggs, cheese, and crunchy bacon, and I damn near have another orgasm. Okay, not really, but it's incredible. Incredible enough I let out a slight moan. Did he really just cook this? I'm so caught up in the moment of enjoying the omelet, I don't realize he sidles up next to me with a plate for him.

His warm breath exhales straight into my ear. "I love when you make that sound but it's usually because I'm inside you."

Heat blooms across my cheeks; they must be ten different shades of pink. How does he still find ways to make me blush? I should see these things coming, but secretly I hope he never stops. I also can't help but notice how he almost sounded jealous of the eggs. He's so damn —I don't know. He's just Deacon. I've never met anyone like him.

"Don't be shy." He digs into his plate, eating faster than I've ever seen anyone eat in my life.

He must catch me staring at him, because he pauses from inhaling his food and asks, "What?" with a mouthful of eggs.

I grin and shake my head. There are no words.

"You've never been in a cafeteria with eighty college football players. You eat when you fucking can or the linemen take all the damn food."

Well, that makes more sense. It also explains a lot of the practical jokes and his sense of humor. Dad always called it locker-room talk.

Deacon resumes annihilating his food, and I can't help but stare at his body. It must take a lot of protein to stay in that type of shape. I'm starting to think his suits don't actually do him justice. All the Collins men are tall, but Deacon is definitely thicker and more muscular than all of them. Football makes sense.

His eyes roll over to meet mine. "What's up?"

"All I can think about is getting you back in bed and getting these off you." I tug on the waistband of his boxers.

He takes a gigantic drink of juice and starts shoveling eggs into his mouth.

I stare at him with wide eyes. His damn fork looks like the Roadrunner's legs.

His hand shoots out with the fork in it and he taps it on my plate. "Eat up." It sounds like a drill instructor barking orders.

I continue to just gape at him.

He stops for a second, turns, and says, "You're gonna need the calories, Quinn."

I shake my head and laugh. "You're crazy."

"Crazy about you."

DEACON

GROANING AND STRETCHING, I move to roll out of bed and realize Quinn's head is on my chest. We took a nap after we finished eating. I look around the room, taking in the scene, and run my fingers through her hair. It's perfect.

Life is perfect.

I lie there, thinking about her living with me. A few months ago, I'd have dry-heaved at the thought of a woman moving in, but now, I think I could get used to waking up next to Quinn every morning.

I pull the sheet back and stare at the curve of her hip pressed up against me. There's a dusting of freckles on her right shoulder. It's impossible to see and not want to kiss them.

My eyes roam to the teeth marks on her left breast. Something primal stirs in me, in the unevolved part of my brain, back when cavemen would mark their territory. It doesn't bother me, though. There's nothing I want more than to protect her—take care of her, even though I know she can fend for herself.

To say I'm turned on right now is the understatement of the century. I'm like a damn addict. Just watching her is like a narcotic flooding my veins.

My cock hardens at the sight of her pale skin and smooth legs. I look at the clock and know her dad probably expects her home soon. I slip out of bed, thinking what I'm about to do might be a mistake, but I can't stop myself. I snatch her phone off the coffee table and press the call button.

"Hello." His voice is gruff.

"Mr. Richards, it's Deacon Collins."

"Is Quinn okay?"

"She's fine. I just wanted to let you know she fell asleep. I know she's normally home by now. I didn't want you to worry, but if there's anything you need, I'll do whatever I can."

"I'm good for a few more hours."

"Great. Thank you, sir." I end the call and grab a glass of water then slide back into bed.

Quinn rolls to her side, hugging my pillow. The urge to reach out and touch her is unbearable and I give in. I trace her curves with the tip of my index finger, down her hip toward her thigh, inching my way between her legs. She's about to get the wake-up call of her life; a Deacon Collins alarm clock special.

I can't imagine what it'd be like to sink my cock into her every morning.

It'd be perfect. We'd get up and fuck. Go to work, come home, have dinner, and fuck again.

I take one of her nipples between my fingers and slide

my head down her stomach. She needs to know what it's like to wake up to my tongue every morning.

I don't make it down in time.

Quinn lets out a soft yawn and her eyes flutter open. They dart down and land on my head between her thighs, staring back up at her.

"Hi," she whispers.

"Hi." I slide back up and brush some hair from her cheek. "Sleep good?"

"Like a baby. I think I'm in love with your bed." She stretches her arms up behind her head.

I take the opportunity to grab her wrists and pin them there. We sit there a moment, faces inches apart. I want to ask her if that's all she loves, my bed, but I choke the words down. It's way too soon for that kind of talk.

"What time is it?" Her eyes widen with panic etched across her face.

"Five-thirty."

"Shit!" She breaks free and shoves past me. Her feet drop to the floor. "I need to get going. My dad."

I watch her from the bed. "Don't worry." I hook my arms around her waist and pull her back into the covers with me. "He's fine. I called him."

Quinn's eyes turn into two huge orbs. "You called him?" Then, a smile spreads across her face. "And how'd that go?"

I shrug like it was no biggie. "He said he's good for an hour or two."

Quinn falls into my arms and breathes a sigh of relief.

I rest my chin on her shoulder where it meets her neck.

"You two besties now? Should I worry you'll be

texting and trading football stories?" She laughs at herself and I love hearing that sound. The sound of her happiness.

"Come here," I growl. "We only have two hours and I don't know if we'll have enough time."

Her eyebrows rise as her head falls back on my chest. "Time for what?"

"Time to fuck each other with our mouths."

She squeals my name as I flip her over. "Deacon!"

"Got something against a proper sixty-nine?" I lean down and capture her nipple between my teeth.

She lets out a soft moan, more like a purr, and my cock hardens at the sound. I go back and forth between her tits trying to decide which one I like best. It's an impossible chore. I tease her repeatedly until she spreads her legs and says, "Fine. Do what you must, sir. I'll endure it."

"I like when you call me sir. Makes me feel powerful and shit."

"Does it now?"

"Goddamn right it does." I roll next to her, abandoning the idea of taking my time. I can't keep my hands off her. "I need you here."

She squeals when I grip her hips and yank her to my mouth. She's facing away from me and straddling my face. I exhale warm breath across her clit, knowing it'll drive her crazy. Like I expected, her thighs quiver against my cheeks.

Her pussy lowers to my mouth, and I dig my fingers into her thighs so she can't scurry away if things get too intense. I bury my tongue in her, licking, sucking, and teasing.

Soft coos of approval fall from her lips, and then I feel her mouth on me.

"Fuck."

She stops to say something, and I fight the urge to grab her head and shove her back down. "Sounds like I'm doing a good job on my end."

I laugh. "Oh, you want this to be a competition?"

"First one to come loses."

"Deal." I smack her on the ass playfully to seal the agreement.

Her lips meet my cock once more, and I already know I'm at risk of losing this bet. Her hot mouth sucks around my shaft taking me as far as she can.

I flatten my tongue on her pussy and tease her clit with the tip of my tongue. She squirms immediately and her cheeks suck tighter around me.

This is heaven. Pure fucking heaven right here.

I always operated under the assumption I could eat pussy better than I could play football, but Quinn is a worthy opponent.

I sink a finger inside her while I tongue her clit. The angle damn near makes my hand cramp up, but I'm not about to lose. Her wetness streams down her thighs and lands on my tongue and she tastes like…mine.

All fucking mine.

It does nothing but fuel me, and I speed up the tempo. Her legs tremble, more and more, amping up in intensity, and I know she's fucking close. I slide a finger down to collect some lube from her hot cunt, then tease the rim of her ass with it.

Her hips start to buck, and I know I have this thing

won now. In fact, I'm so confident, I take my mouth from her for a moment to do a little mid-game shit talking. "It's all over for you, Quinn." I watch my finger press tighter against her and smile when she shakes even harder at the sensation. "Who knew the innocent girl at the office was such a filthy little slut in the bedroom."

She always comes fast when I talk dirty to her.

I hum against her clit and tease both of her holes.

Her pussy clenches tight around my finger and I can tell she's fighting it back with everything she has. Her hips buck against my mouth until she's full on fucking my face and fingers. I love every second of it. I add a second finger to her pussy and tease her ass with my thumb.

One day I'll fuck her there.

Suddenly, I notice I've been so concentrated on pleasing her, I didn't realize my own hips were thrusting up and down, fucking her mouth.

"Dea-con." She pulls her mouth away from my dick, and her entire body quakes. "Oh God."

I yank her into me, and the orgasm pulses through her, from her hips down to her curled toes. She's like a live wire, short-circuiting all over the place.

While she rides my face, my balls lift high and tight.

Uh oh! What the hell?

Then, I feel it. Her fingers, stroking my cock up and down. Everything goes blurry for a split second, almost like an out-of-body experience, then I blow all over her hand.

I can't stop panting. Two-a-day practices in hundred-degree weather my whole life, and I've never been as spent as I am right now. Just as I'm catching my breath, Quinn's mouth is on my cock.

I lean out around her ass and she's cleaning me up with her tongue. I already have the urge to fuck her again. I'm not going soft anytime soon, not with her licking around my shaft.

"I'd call it a draw."

She doesn't see me watching her, and she smiles against my dick. "I was still going after you tapped out."

"Oh bullshit. Remind me to have cameras installed. In case we need an official review in the future to keep you from cheating."

"I'm sure that's exactly why you'd want a camera in here."

I grin. Fuck, she's perfect.

I'm nowhere near done with her, so I flip her around and lift her on top of me.

She doesn't miss a beat. Her hot pussy slides down on my cock, and I nearly lose it. God, she's so hot and wet. I'm not wearing a condom and I never imagined her feeling this goddamn amazing.

She starts to move up and down, but I grip her by the hips and stop her. I stare up into her eyes. "You sure?"

Her cheeks flush and she nods.

Holy fuck.

Quinn takes me all the way to the base, and I groan when she squeezes tight around me. It's so much better this way, bare, skin to skin. I palm her ass and spread her cheeks apart. After her little show earlier, I'm not about to let up on pressing that button. I slip my pinky up against her puckered ass as she rides me. It doesn't take long.

Another orgasm rocks through her. It's so intense I can barely hang on.

Her hot pussy clenches around me, and without the condom between us I don't know how much more I can take. Everything about her intensifies to eleven.

She doesn't know, but Quinn's the only woman I've ever fucked without protection. In a way, I feel like she's my first. It's so much more than sex. It's real and passionate and emotional. It's everything, and I can't let go of it now that I've experienced it with her.

My eyes roll back in my head and I want to come inside her so bad it aches down to my bones. I hold back, knowing I shouldn't.

My brain goes to war, because I don't want to fucking hold back. I want it more than anything I've ever wanted in my life. The thought alone should terrify me, but with Quinn it feels so fucking right and the rest of the world fades away, leaving nothing but the two of us here in this moment.

I lean up and push her back, breaking our connection for a split-second before I slide right back in.

Her ankles hook around my waist and I slant over her mouth and kiss the shit out of her. I know I said I'm possessive, that Quinn is mine, but she owns me just as much, if not more. Nothing has ever felt more right than this, than us.

Our tongues intertwine as I take her as deep as I can. Our foreheads press together, and I lock eyes with her. I swear I can see everything about her in them, all her thoughts and feelings, her goals and desires.

I slide into her over and over, long deep strokes. She

gives me everything I want and more. Things I never knew I wanted or needed but I want and need them from her.

Only her.

So.

Fucking.

Intense.

I bite down on her shoulder as my balls tighten. The war rages in my brain as an orgasm inches up my shaft, but at the last second, I pull out and come all over her stomach. Using the head of my cock, I sign my name in it, right there on her belly, my eyes never leaving hers.

Through my rough pants, the only word that escapes my lips is, "Mine."

Quinn hooks her arms around my neck, pulling my mouth to hers for a kiss.

After we catch our breaths, I grin down lazily at her flushed expression. "We need a shower. You can't go home like this."

We both laugh while she shakes her head.

"Definitely not. I don't care how good you were at football."

It's hard as hell to keep my hands off her in the shower. It's equally difficult to keep my dick from getting hard, but I know if I touch her right now it'll send me on a mission to convince her to spend the night. That's a position I refuse to put her in, regardless of how many positions I'd like to put her in. Her dad needs her, and she has to get home.

I know without a doubt I'll be jerking off later to the image of her all soaped up in my shower.

Once we're toweled off and dressed, and it's time for her to leave, I pull her back one more time for a kiss. Who am I kidding? I pull her back four times, promising each one is the last. I can't remember ever feeling this carefree in my life. Colors are more vibrant and sounds more vivid. It feels like I'm floating in the clouds, completely weightless.

She breaks away from my last kiss far too soon.

My hands instinctively roam her hips.

"Deacon, I gotta go." She pulls away, still grinning.

"Text me when you get home."

"I will." She stops to get on the elevator, but before I close my door, she sprints back for one more kiss, then finally breaks free and leaves.

When she disappears into the elevator an emptiness settles over me and I don't like it at all.

She's the only one who can soothe this ache deep inside me. Not seeing her face is torture.

My phone rings from the other room and it's a welcome distraction from thinking about Quinn walking away. I jog back to the bedroom and Rick Lawrence's name lights up on the screen.

About fucking time.

I've been waiting on this call. I swipe my finger across the screen and place the phone next to my ear. "Tell me something good, bitch."

"Better than good. We need to meet."

"The Gage?" It's a restaurant with a nice bar over by

Millennium Park. Everyone from the office hangs out there after work sometimes.

"Fifteen minutes."

"Perfect timing. See you there."

———

I HOP out of a cab on Michigan Avenue, across the street from the park. I didn't feel like driving and parking downtown, and I wanted to be able to think freely about Quinn without dealing with traffic. Walking through the glass door, I spot Rick at the bar knocking back a rocks glass that's most likely filled with expensive whiskey.

I take the stool next to him and order a scotch.

He doesn't say a word, just slides a file in front of me. "I smell virgin pussy in my future."

Jesus, this guy.

I crane my head around to make sure nobody is within earshot.

Rick grins wide as hell but stares straight ahead, clearly amused with how uncomfortable he makes people. The guy has no filter. It's one thing to talk that way with the guys in a fucking locker room, but he lets it fly no matter where he's at.

"Depends on what you have here." I flip through the folder and my eyes widen. My hands speed up on the papers, my eyes scanning the pages. "Fuck, can I use any of this? How the hell did you get it?"

"First, we have something more important to discuss."

"Okay?"

"I saw Donavan looking at my sweet, innocent Mary the other day. You're going to take care of that, right?"

I wave a flippant hand in his direction, my eyes still roaming the evidence he brought. "Yeah, yeah. Consider it done. Can I fucking use this shit?"

"All admissible. Didn't have to do anything shady."

I turn and give him a stare that says *don't fuck with me*.

He holds both hands up and laughs. "I'm not bullshitting. Nobody knows. I kept up my end of the bargain."

I slide my rocks glass over and bump his with it, unable to peel my eyes away from the documents in front of me. "I'll talk to Donavan." There's no way I'll talk to Donavan, because then he might actually take an interest if he knows there's competition. I already know there's no way in hell he wants Mary and her ankle-length skirts. I'm sure he just glanced in her direction or ordered her to do something for him.

Rick knocks back his whiskey and stands up. "Well then, I gotta go to mass or whatever it's called. Have to get right with the Lord. Jesus won't be the only one getting nailed in church this week." He tosses me a grin and heads out before I can reply to his blasphemy.

My eyes glance once more to the papers. I'm about to score a game-winning touchdown for the firm, and I'm going to rub that shit right in Tecker's smug faces.

DEACON

It's early Monday morning and I couldn't feel better.

Dr. James Flynn stands in front of the building as I hop out of a cab.

"Mr. Flynn."

"Deacon." He reaches out and shakes my hand.

Dude has a decent grip for being in his sixties. He looks confused.

I hold up the file Rick gave me. "It'll all make sense in a minute. Thanks for coming on such short notice."

We walk into the building and head to the receptionist's desk.

Dr. Flynn's eyes roam around, taking in the surroundings. "Why are we meeting at her lawyer's office?"

"I'm about to put this whole ordeal behind us. Trust me."

"Can I help you?" asks the receptionist.

"We have a meeting with Chauncey." He's the lawyer representing the woman who accused Dr. Flynn.

"Oh yes, right this way."

She leads us down a long hallway, the clacking of her heels amplified by the tile and twelve-foot ceiling. At the end, we walk into a conference room surrounded by four glass walls.

It's nice, but not as nice as my firm's building. Their shit is on the first floor, and I'm about to remind Chauncey and his client they fucked with the wrong people.

"Mr. Collins, Dr. Flynn." Chauncey shakes both our hands. He's about Dr. Flynn's age and probably thinks he's about to steamroll a young hotshot attorney into a settlement.

I told him on the phone we were ready to talk about making a deal, but it was really just laying a trap for an ambush.

His client sits there with a cocky grin on her face. I can practically see the dollar signs in her eyes.

Despite that, I can't help but notice Dr. Flynn doesn't look angry. He has no idea what I have in my file, but he doesn't look emotional at all. His demeanor is friendly even.

Fuck, this guy has way more composure than I do. If some woman tried to ruin my career I'd burn her house to the ground. There's no way I'd smile and be nice. I wouldn't even pretend.

We all sit down, and Chauncey starts in, "So, we have matters to discuss."

"Yes, we do." I pull the manila folder out and set it in front of me.

Every eye in the room lands on it.

"What's that?" asks Chauncey.

"Just some research." I open it up and rifle through the pages, pretending to read them even though I have them pretty much memorized. "Has your client ever lived in Phoenix?"

The smug grin disappears from her face, and her eyes widen.

"Maybe worked for a…" I pause, for dramatic effect. "Dr. Lancaster?"

Now, her face turns red with rage. Her entire body tenses and her hands grip the arms of her chair.

"What is this?" Chauncey reaches over for her forearm. "I thought we were discussing a settlement?"

I ignore his question and keep going, staring right at her. "Of course, you weren't using the name Bridgette Smith at that time, were you? How about New Orleans and a Dr. Markwardt? That ring a bell?"

Chauncey looks at Bridgette, then back at me. "What's going on here?"

"Well, it seems your client has a pattern. Job as a nurse. Sexual harassment suit. Payday. Moves on when the money runs out, I'm guessing. It's a clever little cycle, until you get caught."

"Let me see those."

I slide the papers over to him but keep some in front of me.

He fumbles through the pages. "Even if you can prove this is her, it doesn't mean your client didn't do what she's accused him of."

Bridgette, or whatever her real name is, perks up in her seat, like maybe there's still some hope.

Surprisingly, Dr. Flynn remains calm and collected,

ALEX WOLF & SLOANE HOWELL

like he doesn't have a care in the world. He hasn't said a word and hasn't looked worried the entire time this case has developed. All he ever insisted on was a fair defense, from the beginning.

I glare at the woman across from me, because the shit she does undermines every real victim of harassment and sexual assault and makes it difficult for them to come forward. There's a fear they won't be believed, because it's rare for concrete evidence to be present in these cases. Not to mention, I just don't like her.

"Let me just squash any hope you have of getting paid today." I keep my eyes locked on her. "These..." I slide more papers out into the middle of the table. "Are text messages to and from your friend, Crystal."

Her face heats up again and her jaw sets firm. She knows I have her.

"If you'd kept quiet, we might be cutting you a check. But you had to go brag, didn't you? And I'm guessing, since you like to screw people over, none of your friends are actually loyal friends. Yet, you spilled your guts to Crystal about how you were about to get a huge settlement from Dr. Flynn." I slide another sheet of paper out. "This is a sworn affidavit from Crystal stating you also told her you made it all up. You can read it if you want. You go into a lot of detail."

I push the papers toward her and she shoves them back at me.

I snicker and gesture toward the affidavit. "Know what that cost me? All your messages and emails and that affidavit?"

Bridgette glares. "I don't know. What?"

"Five hundred bucks. That's how easy your friend rolled over on you."

"Well, I think we all need to step back a moment..." Chauncey backpedals in a hurry. I can't tell if he's pissed or embarrassed by us blindsiding him.

"That won't be necessary." All eyes go to Dr. Flynn. He stares right at Bridgette.

She's moved past anger, and I swear it looks like she's about to cry now. It has to be an act. She's a damn con artist.

Dr. Flynn looks across the table at her with soft eyes. "Do you still want your job at the hospital?"

What the fuck?

I put a hand on his arm. "Doctor, I would strongly advise—"

He holds up his other hand to cut me off, but doesn't break eye contact with her. "Would you like your job back, Bridgette?"

The tears flow down her cheeks and she sniffles. "Yes, please. I'm sorry."

"Well, then. It looks like we have a settlement after all." He stands from his chair, walks around the large conference table, and holds his hand out in front of her. "See you at work Monday."

She looks up at him and takes his hand, nodding. "Yes. I-I'll be there."

"Sounds great. Can't wait to have you back." He looks at me and gestures with his head toward the door. "Let's go, son."

I don't know what the fuck just happened, but I gather up everything and head out with him. We make our way to the front of the building and I turn to face him.

"I have to advise that this is a terrible idea. I mean, I would understand if you don't want to go after her for defamation of character, but hiring her back..."

"Did you see that woman in there?"

I shrug. "Sure."

He sighs. "She didn't just start doing the things she does one day out of the blue. Someone taught it to her. She grew up with that. It's all she knows."

"I mean, okay? That's not a good reason to ruin people's lives for her own gain. Have you seen the things they've said about you on the internet? Even when we dismiss this case, the stigma will still be there. It's all over Twitter. 'High profile heart surgeon sexually assaults nurse.' All it takes is being accused. They won't publicize them dropping the suit because it's boring. It'll be back-page news."

"Do you have good parents? Do they love you unconditionally?"

What the hell is he talking about? "Sure. I mean, my mom would tell us she loved us no matter what. I always knew my dad felt that way, even if he didn't say it."

He points back at the building. "She's never known that. She's never had anyone care about her, even after she made a mistake. This is an opportunity to show her what that's like. If she continues the same behavior, then so be it. But I won't be the one who perpetuates it."

"I just... Okay. Fine. You're the client. If that's what you want to do, go for it."

I sigh.

He puts a hand on my shoulder. "You're a good kid, Deacon. It's why I like you. I can see you care about those close to you and your clients more than you care about money. I know you think you're looking out for me, and I appreciate that. People need to step back and see the big picture, though, before rushing to condemn someone. Nobody is perfect, I don't care who you are." He stares off across the street. "God knows I'm not, even if I didn't do this. The world needs a lot more empathy and a lot less judgment."

He climbs into a cab and I wave. It wasn't exactly how I saw this thing playing out, but it's still a win for the firm. Also, in roughly a decade of being a lawyer, I don't think I've ever seen anything like that happen.

Regardless, I can't wait to see Tecker's face when I shove this up their ass.

QUINN

I CAN'T STOP GLOWING from my time with Deacon. It's nothing like what I expected a relationship with him would be like. He leaves me breathless with the things he says and the sweet things he does.

I still can't believe he called Dad to check in on him. I mean, who the hell does that? I can't remember any guy I've dated taking that kind of initiative. The old man was impressed.

Like it wasn't already bad enough he worships Deacon as a football god. Dad keeps mumbling things like, "That boy is perfect."

The funny thing is, I can't argue with him.

He freaking cooked for me!

Maybe I'm a little jaded from years of preparing every meal, but I can't remember a man ever cooking for me, other than Dad, and that seems like ages ago.

My only complaint about the weekend is it went by too fast. I didn't want it to end. I spent most of yesterday studying and texting back and forth with Heather. She must've thought I was insane, because I never share intimate details of my dating life, not even with her.

But I couldn't help myself. Maybe I've never opened up to her because I've never dated anyone worth mentioning. I didn't share everything, of course, but I'm pretty sure I gushed non-stop to the point she likely rolled her eyes and wanted the conversation over. It was payback for all the times she's done it to me.

Now, it's Monday, and I'm already looking forward to Friday.

I get to my desk and don't even have to look; the sound of Tate's heels clacking on the floor is unmistakable. I glance in that direction just in time to catch her curly blonde head of hair turn the corner. I swear she's always so put together and dresses like she stepped out of a fashion spread in a magazine.

She starts to pass me, then stops, turns, and smirks. "Someone had a good weekend."

How the hell does she do that?

I must've been cheesing like a fool at my desk. Yes, Tate, it was in fact the best weekend I've had in a long time. I still can't believe I had unprotected sex with Deacon Collins. He's the first man I've ever let do that. I'm on birth control and he pulled out, but pregnancy isn't something I want to worry about anytime soon.

It was so damn intense, bare, skin to skin. I'm pretty sure I could have sex with him twenty-four seven the rest of my life and die happy. I'd probably live to be a hundred. Sometimes I feel like sex is all I think about now that I'm with him.

I'm with him.

Shit, Tate's still standing there.

"It was kind of perfect. How was yours?"

"Crazy. I spent both days with a wedding planner and centerpieces." She rolls her eyes.

I kind of feel sorry for the wedding planners. I wouldn't expect Tate to be a bridezilla because she's nuts about her wedding being perfect, I'd expect her to be one because she's nuts about *everything* in her life being perfect.

"Well, you only do it once." Hopefully.

"If I'd known it would eat so much time, I might've suggested we elope instead." She takes a deep breath and it's rare for her to look flustered. "It's all to spend the rest of my life with Decker. That's the only thing that keeps me from shoving a candelabra up someone's ass." She gets this faraway look in her eyes, though, when she mentions Decker. I want that for me.

Could I have that with Deacon? *Do* I already have that look with Deacon?

The answer in my mind is a resounding yes. I don't even have to think about it.

"You've got it bad," Tate mumbles.

I laugh and the phone rings.

I hold up a finger to Tate and answer. "Decker Collins' office. How may I help you?"

"I need your boss now."

"He's in a meeting. Can I give him a message?"

"Someone at your office fucked up my contract. I only received one percent of the payment. I can't purchase any materials for the job." The angry voice booms on the line and I realize it's one of the Beckley brothers.

"I'll look into it right away, Mr. Beckley. If you could just give me the specifics for Mr. Collins."

I take down the information, and Tate peeks at my notes, clearly taking an interest in what's going on.

I hold up a finger at her as the man screams a few more expletives before slamming the phone down. I feel awful for him but yelling at me won't fix his problem. Decker's going to blow his top when he hears. It won't be pretty around the office.

I cradle the phone and pull the Beckley contract up on my computer. I scan through the pages, looking for the section on payment terms.

Uh oh.

"Erm, Tate...this contract on that hotel renovation. Shouldn't this be ten percent instead of one? I'm no expert or anything but I..." I catch myself before I tell her about my class on contracts at school.

"Let me see it." She spins my monitor toward her, narrowing her eyes on the text I highlighted. "Yep." Her lips mash into a thin line and her jaw flexes. Someone is going to be up shit creek. I would not want to be on the other end of that conversation. Tate writes down something on a Post-it and storms toward Decker's office.

I close out the contract and hope whoever messed this up doesn't get in too much trouble. That's a significant error to overlook, though, and I have no idea how that could happen. There's a review process to prevent these types of things.

I keep myself occupied going through my schedule and making sure I'm ahead on my tasks for the day. I've learned the best thing to do when Decker is on the warpath is to have my head down and look busy. If I can have whatever he's after waiting for him before he asks, even better.

Where the hell is Deacon? He's normally in by now.

My phone buzzes with a text, like he can read my mind.

Deacon: Good morning, beautiful.

I grin at the screen then catch him stepping off the elevator.

I give him a small wave. It's awkward as hell, but he looks so cute with his sheepish grin when he sees me.

He lifts his hand to reciprocate, but immediately drops it when Decker hauls ass toward him.

Oh no.

Deacon, what'd you do?

Maybe Decker's pissed, and just wants to tell Deacon someone made a mistake and he needs to go have them fix it. That has to be it. At least, I hope that's it. It's probably wishful thinking.

The more heated Decker looks, the more my stomach twists into a knot.

Within a few seconds it's clear Deacon handled the contract. I wish I had known it was him. Maybe I could've gone to him after the phone call and given him a chance to correct it before anyone found out. But Tate was right there, and I couldn't lie to her.

Decker and Deacon both stomp toward a conference room once they notice all the associates and paralegals staring at them. What if Decker and Tate tell Deacon I'm the one who told them about the error in the contract?

Say goodbye to this fantastic Monday.

DEACON

I FIRE off a text to Quinn, then walk off the elevator feeling on top of the world. I spot her right as she gets my text and I smile and wave.

I'm a little late getting to the office after my meeting with Dr. Flynn, but I called ahead and told my secretary I'd be in by ten.

It doesn't take long for Decker to ruin my fantastic morning.

He heads right at me with a scowl on his face. "Conference room, now."

I glance around and the entire office stares at us. "Okay." I look back at Quinn, but her head's down. The uneasy look on her face makes me frown.

What the fuck just happened in here? I just won. A huge goddamn win and they're coming at me?

I follow Decker to the conference room and take a seat. Tate walks in a few seconds later.

Fucking wonderful.

"Someone piss in your oatmeal?" I grin.

"How about you explain this to me." Decker slams a contract down on the table.

I glance at it. It's the construction contract for the Beckley brothers. "What about it? Sent that off a long time ago."

"Look. At. It."

"You made a huge error." Tate stares at me with a smug grin, like she's pleased I made a mistake.

I can't think with her eyeing me while I try and read over the contract. My face heats up as I scan the words. I can't believe I just went through all that shit, murdering the Flynn case like a goddamn champion, and they have the balls to sit here and waterboard me over a fucking contract.

Tate lingers closer, almost at my side.

"Jesus Christ, would you get her the fuck out of here, Decker?"

"Excuse me?" Tate starts toward me like she might get in my face, all five foot nothing of her in heels.

I glare back at her. "You heard me. I don't need you running your yap at me non-stop. This shit doesn't concern you."

Her hands go to her hips. "I'm a partner just like you. Everything concerns me."

"Yeah, you had to fuck the boss to get the title, too. Now, what? You fucked Donavan over and that wasn't good enough? You gotta start in on me?"

"You little motherfucker." She takes off toward me once more and Decker grabs her by the waist and yanks her back. She doesn't stop yelling at me over his shoulder.

"You had to share a mom with the boss to get your title, you ungrateful little—"

Decker puts himself between us and wheels around on her, then glares back at me. His face is fire-engine red. "Enough! Goddamn it!" He paces back and forth and clutches his temple like he might have an aneurysm. "Both of you are giving me a fucking headache with your crybaby bullshit."

Tate glares at me. I knew I'd hit a nerve, but I don't give a shit. She's not even thirty and struts around like she's a fucking manager. She ran off to Decker and made him drop Donavan's suit against one of her clients. Decker did exactly what she told him to do. He's like a puppy following her ass around.

Pussy-whipped bastard. It'd be understandable if she was cool like Quinn, but I don't know what the fuck he sees in her. Every once in a while, I think we're on good terms, then she does shit like this. Decker and Donavan barely talk anymore. She's ripping our family apart.

My hands ball into fists, and I know I need to keep my shit together and just ignore Tate and fix the problem. I'd love to throw the Flynn case right back at them, but they won't care. They only focus on the fuck-ups when it comes to me. Everything else gets swept under the rug or glossed over. I won't give them the satisfaction of downplaying my success.

I take a few deep breaths and skim over the contract, finally able to think. It doesn't take long to spot the mistake.

Yeah, I fucked up. So what? I typed one percent instead of ten. It's my fault. I know it is. It wouldn't have been a big deal if I hadn't ignored the review process and sent it through. It's no excuse for them to scold me like a child instead of treating me like an adult colleague.

I shake my head. Jesus, the one time I skip a step, this shit happens. It's like the universe hates me.

"I'll take care of it."

Decker takes a step toward me. Clearly, he's not going to let me do my job and fix the problem without running his mouth about how irresponsible I am. "Do you know how much money this cost a brand-new client? He's pissed and threatening litigation."

"Fuck, I said I'd fix it. Calm down and I'll smooth it over."

Tate pops off from the corner of the room. "I'm not comfortable with him doing—"

I cut her off, speaking through gritted teeth. "Decker, if you don't shut her up, I'm going to choke slam her on this table Undertaker-style."

Decker's eyes get wide and he shoots a glare at Tate like, *I don't know if he's serious, but please just shut up for five seconds.*

His scowl returns when he turns back to me. "This is rookie shit, Deacon. You shouldn't have been making changes on this contract. You should've been reviewing the fucking thing after an associate handled it."

"You done yet? I'll fucking fix it. How many times do I need to say it?"

"Oh yeah, maybe you should have your girlfriend review it this time around. She's the one who found your mistake." His words are like a slap to my face.

What the hell was Quinn doing looking at my

contracts? Then she ran off to Tate and Decker and ratted me out?

"The fuck did you say?" When I glance up, I see something I don't expect.

Tate's practically shooting lasers out her eyes, but they're aimed right at Decker. Her gaze rolls back over to me and her eyes soften. It's maybe the kindest look she's ever given me.

I shake my head. I don't need this shit. I don't want Tate's goddamn pity, either.

Decker doesn't know when to quit, though. It's his opportunity to pile it on and he doesn't miss a beat. "Maybe we should give her your office. Put you out on the phones and running errands."

He's taking this shit too far, and I can't bottle the rage coursing through my veins any longer.

I fly out of my chair.

Tate's eyes bug out of her head.

In two long strides, I'm right in Decker's grill. "Keep pushing me." I lean in so close we're inches apart. "I fucking dare you."

Decker gulps a little. We're about the same height but I have at least thirty pounds on him and didn't play a pussy sport like baseball. He takes a step back and waves me off with a flippant hand, trying to save face. "Just get it handled, goddamn it."

"Yeah." I glare at both of them then step into the hall before I do something ridiculous like throw Decker through the window. I can't remember ever being this angry and I don't like it. It's not me. My chest heaves up and down and I want to rip the fucking walls of this place down.

I don't even have a bad temper, but when he mentioned Quinn I just about lost my shit. I've never felt this way, never flown off the handle like that. I need to get out of this place for a while. Just to calm down.

As soon as I walk past Quinn's desk, Dexter appears right next to me. "Drinks tonight at The Gage, you in? I'm taking out some new girls from the Dallas office." He punches me in the shoulder, oblivious to what just went down.

I scowl at Quinn and she shrinks back in her seat.

I don't even know why, but without thinking I say, "Yeah. I'll be there."

Her face pales, and I immediately regret the words, but I'm too pissed to talk to her right now. I'll say things I don't mean, like I just did. I need to get away from everyone.

Fuck. I hate Tecker. I hate the whole world right now. Most of all I hate myself because I know I just hurt Quinn.

I didn't just hurt her. I could tell by the look on her face, I crushed her.

I head to my office feeling like the world's biggest asshole.

I've never seen anyone make a situation better when they're pissed off.

I get to my desk and flop down in my chair. It's not like the problem is hard to solve. Add a goddamn zero and draft a new contract, kiss a little ass and wipe my hands of this mess.

Fuck the client for not reading the shit he signed

anyway. I could never say that to his face, but he's the biggest dumb fuck in this whole ordeal. Who signs something they haven't read?

I drop my head into my hands and close my eyes.

Quinn.

Why did I say that shit in front of her? Am I sabotaging myself? She didn't deserve that. I don't even know what really happened and now she probably hates me.

I just don't understand. If she knew, why didn't she come to me? Why go behind my back to Tate and Decker?

I know Tate and Quinn are friends, but Quinn knows I don't get along with her. She knows every detail about every person in the office. She's well aware how my brothers—outside of Decker—feel about Kim Jong Tate.

Regardless, I can't focus on my personal shit right now. I have to get this contract situation smoothed over in a hurry. Quinn will have to wait, and it'll do some good to step back like Dr. Flynn said. Empathize instead of judge.

That's what I need to do.

QUINN

I DON'T KNOW if I've ever felt as stupid as I do right now. I thought Deacon cared about me; we were moving forward and starting a serious relationship that meant something to him. Meant something to both of us.

Maybe it was all me and I was seeing what I wanted to see or building up a fantasy in my head that didn't reflect reality.

The Deacon I was with all day Saturday isn't the Deacon who showed up after he left the conference room.

I can't breathe. My chest burns and my stomach twists into a pretzel. Was it all a game? Was he building me up just to rip my heart out?

"Just the person I was looking for." Decker smiles.

Tate shoots him a death stare that even makes my fingers tremble.

"Oh yeah?" I squeak the words out and my throat burns tight.

Tears attempt to gather in the corners of my eyes, and I fight them back. I won't cry in front of my boss. I can't break, but all I want to do is crumble right here on the spot. Deacon's words play on a loop through my head and I can't rid the dark expression in his eyes from my brain.

"What's wrong?" He shoots Tate a *what the fuck* look, but she ignores him. "I'll, uhh, come back."

When he's gone, Tate grabs me by the shoulders. "Let's go to my office."

I nod, biting back my tears. I don't know if I'm about to cry because I'm pissed and want to punch Deacon in the balls or because I'm hurt. Maybe it's a little of both. This is exactly what I was afraid would happen. He'd get me to trust him. I'd let him in, and he'd jump on the first opportunity to crush me.

He can have his drinks with the new employees from Dallas. I won't be sitting around waiting for his empty promises.

It will pass.

I feel completely empty, like a shell. Used? Confused? I want to hit something.

Tate leads me to the leather couch in her office. I'm too upset to sit but I do it anyway to keep myself from going after Deacon and screaming in his face. My bottom lip quivers and I sink my teeth into it, trying anything that might replace the pain in my heart. It doesn't help. I don't think anything will.

"Quinn," Tate whispers. "I'm sorry."

"Why are you sorry? You didn't do anything, did you?"

"Decker wasn't supposed to bring your name up. He told me he wouldn't but the two egomaniacs in there got pissed off at each other, and personal shit started flying around the room. You did the right thing pointing it out." She reaches out for my hand. "You know how they get. It was ugly and I'm sure Deacon didn't mean whatever he said out there just now. He's pissed off and embarrassed."

"Makes two of us."

Tate did her job, but I feel betrayed by her too. She told Decker about me and Deacon. I know how Decker is when he gets pissed.

I'm sure he loved rubbing Deacon's nose in the mud, just because he could. "Maybe I should look for a job somewhere else."

"That seems pretty hasty." Tate leans back, clearly surprised.

"Tate, I've been going to law school at night for three years. I'm almost finished."

Her frown turns to a smile. "Really? Good for you. That's awesome."

"I keep thinking. You know how it'll look if I'm dating a partner when I'm done. People will think I slept my way into a position I didn't earn. I've worked so hard for this firm."

"If anyone can relate, I can. I had to scratch and claw for everything I have. I'd probably tell you to do just that; go to another firm and start fresh, but we need you here. You're irreplaceable. I have no doubt you'll be a great attorney."

"Nobody will look at me as anything but Decker's glorified assistant and Deacon's ex-girlfriend."

Tate huffs out a long sigh. "You have to do what's best for you. There are plenty of great firms out there and I'll personally write you a letter of recommendation. But right now, don't do anything sudden. Men expect us to act emotionally because that's all they think we are, a big ball of emotions waiting to explode. Step back and get out of your head. Make sound, logical decisions. Sit down and do what you do best; analyze. Trust me. I've been there."

I nod. I know she's right. When men act petty or get angry, everyone just brushes it off. Like Decker and Deacon fighting like children in the conference room. It won't be brought up in reviews or management discussions. But everyone remembers when a woman does it and she's seen as a time bomb waiting to go off. "I'll think about it."

"It'll be a real shame if we lose you. I mean that as a colleague and as a friend."

"Thanks."

"Anytime." She glances at her watch. "Why don't you take an early lunch. Let the temperature cool a little around here."

I leave her office feeling a bit better, but I still can't shake Deacon's hateful stare from my mind. I walk past his office and start to knock but my pride won't let me. I didn't do anything wrong. If his first reaction is to throw other women in my face instead of talking to me like an adult, he's not mature enough for a relationship.

Tears burn in my eyes once more when I pass the supply closet. Our closet.

I do need to get the hell out of here for a while. I make it to my desk and fire off a text to Heather asking if she can meet for lunch.

QUINN

IT'S BEEN two days and I can't stop thinking about Deacon. I miss him more than I should. More than I realized I ever could. I miss his smile and his random texts. I miss him yanking me into the closet.

Neither of us have made an attempt to reach out, and he hasn't been in the office. I have no idea if he went out for drinks with Dexter or not. I tell myself I don't care, but I do. Which eats me up because I don't have time to worry about him or be jealous.

I have school and my father to think about. The one thing I'm certain of is I'm glad I listened to Tate about taking my time to think things through. I haven't decided what to do about my job yet. I would love to resign if Dad and I could afford it. It would free up time to be home with him and study.

It makes me hate Decker even more for paying me so well. I'm dependent on him now. I have to think about our bills and Dad's medical care. However, I know I'll never be taken seriously at The Hunter Group. I'll always be the girl who hooked up with Deacon Collins in the supply closet and slept her way to the top, or the girl who was the best at fetching Decker's coffee.

Even if it's not true, perception trumps reality, always. Once people know Deacon and I were together, it'll be all anyone talks about at the office. I could transfer to Dallas, but then I'd have to move Dad across the country. There's no way in hell he'd go for that. He's a Chicagoan, born and bred.

My chest squeezes tight at the thought of Deacon and I let out a sigh.

Dad glances over at me. "What's the matter, kiddo?" His eyes crinkle at the sides, showing his age.

I haven't said anything to him about Deacon. Regardless of how pissed I am, I can't bring myself to say anything bad about him. I don't know if it's to protect Dad or Deacon. Probably both. I can't keep this charade up forever, though. My dad can read me better than anyone.

I get about halfway through the story and trail off, no longer wanting to think about everything. It hurts too much.

My dad snickers.

I glare at him. "Why are you laughing?" How is any of this remotely funny to him? Can't he see I'm hurting and conflicted? My damn life is at a crossroads and I have no idea what I should do.

"I'm not laughing at you. I just remember those feelings."

"Huh?"

"Being in love."

I roll my eyes. "I am *not* in love."

"Sure." He snickers again.

My face heats up, but deep down I know he's right. I do love Deacon and that's why this hurts so damn bad.

Dad gets this far off look in his eye, like he's reliving the past. "When I met your mom, she was the prettiest thing I'd ever seen. She had your big green eyes. Of course, back then I still had my red hair." He pats his bald head and laughs.

I smile.

He never talks about my mom…about before.

"I made a lot of mistakes with her. But God did I love her and wish I could've been the man she wanted me to be. I miss that feeling. I miss her smile and sometimes I see it when you laugh."

"You think she ever thinks about us?" I've never allowed myself to truly miss her. I mean, you can't miss something you never had, but I had a small sliver of Deacon and I miss him so damn much.

The jerk.

"Maybe. I know I think about her and wonder if I should have gone after her. Or asked her to stay. Things were complicated, kiddo. She had dreams she wanted to go after, and she did. I think I got the better end of the deal." He winks at me.

"Gee, thanks." I nudge him with my elbow.

"Do you love this guy? Be honest with yourself."

For some reason, everything crashes into me at once. Maybe it's just me admitting to myself I'm in love, and all the hurt that follows knowing he must not feel the same way. He'd have come after me already. My hands shoot up to cover my face and tears stream down my cheeks as I nod at my dad.

"Oh, sweetie." He wraps an arm around my shoulder, and I collapse right into him.

He smooths the hair on my head as I cry into his shoulder. When I finally rise, he's smiling.

"God, I really wish you would stop smiling at me right now."

"Oh, honey. It's not because you're having problems with the guy, or because you're hurting. I know you're in pain."

"What is it then?"

"It's because I haven't been able to do this in years."

"Do what?"

"Be the one taking care of you."

Well, if I was crying hard before, the floodgates open up now.

"And don't worry. I've got a shotgun shell down there with Deacon's name written all over it. I don't care how good he was at football; nobody messes with my baby girl."

"Thanks, Daddy." I curl up into his side again.

"Joking aside, sweetheart. I've seen the way that boy looks at you. You may not think it, but he's suffering right now. Bad. Trust me, I know things."

"I don't know what to do. It's complicated. He probably hates me."

"As much as I still dislike some of your mother's choices, I still love her. I think I always will. Finish law school and go work at a different firm. He'll come running, begging for forgiveness."

"When did you get so wise?"

Dad belts out a laugh. "I'm not wise. Just been through a lot of shit. Experience has its merits."

I shake my head at him. This talk was nice, and I feel a little better.

My heart hurts a little less.

But I still miss Deacon and I can't see that feeling ever going away.

DEACON

"Good job getting that contract shit squared away. I know you've been working around the clock. Everyone was happy with the terms. Don't fucking do it again." Decker semi-smiles at me as his eyes dart over to a picture of him and Tate. After a few long seconds he says, "It may have been a mistake to bring up Quinn. And I shouldn't have said all that other shit."

I smirk. "Almost sounds like an apology." Yeah, I did work my ass off, you prick. I had to draft an entire new contract and get it negotiated between the parties, then had to offer a hundred free legal hours to each of them to keep them from going elsewhere.

"You fucked up. Don't press your luck." He shuffles some papers on his desk and I can't help but glance over at them. He mumbles, "Sorry."

"What was that?"

"Don't make me kick your ass. I'm your big brother; I don't give a fuck how many extra pounds of gut you're rocking under that suit."

"Hard as granite, bitch." I rub my abs and laugh. "I shouldn't have yelled at Tate that way, either. It was purely from a professional standpoint and not personal. But, she's your fiancée and I feel bad about it."

"I appreciate that. It's like a daycare around here trying to deal with all of you."

This is how it's always been between all of us. One minute we're about to fight, the next second we're best friends. It is what it is. Although, Donavan and Decker's little feud is still ongoing and worries the shit out of me.

"By the way, I fixed the Dr. Flynn problem. Would've told you sooner, but you ripped my ass about the contract."

Decker's eyes dart up to mine. "Really? You made it go away?"

"Yeah, I do a lot more than just party with clients. I work hard around here, even if I fuck off sometimes."

"How'd you get it taken care of?"

I tell him everything that happened and by the end he's grinning like a madman.

"Well, fuck. Good work." His eyes roam over to the wall. "Maybe I'm too hard on you sometimes, but it's only because I know how good you could be."

"Yeah. Anyway, I have some shit to take care of." I stand up from the chair.

Decker slides some papers off to the corner of his desk.

I notice Quinn's name and bend down so I can read it.

"Shit." Decker tries to cover it up but I'm faster.

I snatch it off his desk.

"Don't…"

I hold a hand up and start reading. By the end, the

paper is balled up in my fist and my eyes dart around his office.

I haven't spoken to her since everything blew up a few days ago. I know she probably thinks I'm an asshole, but I had to fix this mess and it's taken up all my time. I figured she was mad as fuck and I just didn't know what to say to her. I thought I'd give her a few days to cool off then reach out. But now…

"You weren't supposed to see that." Decker runs a hand through his hair and cups the back of his neck. "God, I wish everyone would keep their personal shit out of the office. I'm no good at dealing with it."

"I'm your brother." I shake the paper in front of his face. "You should have told me Quinn was resigning. Tate told you about us. You know how I feel about her."

"Are you sure she knows how you feel about her?" He glances to the paper in my hand.

I rush out of his office on a goddamn mission, ignoring the question.

Fucking women.

Two days and she already resigned.

I head to her desk and she's not there.

Fuck.

She can run but she can't hide from me forever. The contract shit is done, and I have nothing but time on my hands. We're going to talk about this whether she likes it or not and it's not going to be pretty.

I pause to think through the problem. If anyone knows where she is it'll be her little buddy Tate. This was probably her idea, anyway. I swear that woman wants to ruin my life. If Decker had any clue what was about to happen, it'd be world war three, because I know Tate is still seething from everything I said to her, but I don't give a fuck.

I may have promised to be nice to her, but that was before I knew about this.

I barge into her office without knocking. She ends her phone call and looks up at me with wide eyes. Her face slowly morphs to red and I'm begging for her to give me a reason to take out all this frustration on her.

"Where is she?"

"How about you fuck off out of my office then come back and ask nicely." She folds her hands neatly on her desk and continues to stare at me.

My jaw ticks. Does she really expect me to say please? I've about had it with this chick, but I'll be damned if I don't walk out of her office, swallow my pride and the desire to rip the door off the goddamn hinges. I want answers, and this is the best way to accomplish it, but inside I'm raging. I do my best to hide it behind my eyes and walk back in. "Will you please tell me where Quinn is?"

I expect Tate to laugh hysterically at me, but she doesn't.

What the fuck?

"It's real, isn't it?"

"What? I don't know what you're saying. Can you please just tell me where she is?"

"You're in love with her." She eyes me from head to toe. "Like, batshit crazy in love. I've never seen you look mad a day I've known you, and now you're about to rage on anything in sight."

I stand there, unable to form any words. I just look at the ground and nod.

"You know what, Deacon? You might not believe this, but I actually like you."

"Huh?" I huff out half a laugh. I'm more surprised than anything.

"Yeah. And I think you and Quinn are great for each other. Even though I shouldn't break the girl code, I'm going to tell you where she is. But hear this and listen up. If you piss her off, hurt her more than she's already hurting, I'll take that golf club from your office. You know the one I showed you how to use when I first came to the firm, because you *suck* at golf... remember that?"

I grind my teeth and ignore her insult because I want to know where Quinn is more than anything in the world. "I remember."

"And do you remember all that shit you said to me in the conference room?"

"I'm..."

"Don't apologize for it. You didn't mean any of that shit. You were pissed off at Decker and took it out on me."

"That's correct."

"Okay, so yeah, the golf club..."

"Fuck, I remember, okay? Jesus Christ."

Tate smiles. "Well, you talk to me that way again, or tell Quinn how you found out where she was...I'll shove it so far up your ass it'll knock your goddamn head to the eighteenth green. We clear?"

"Yeah, yeah. I get it. You're a badass and I'm an asshole, so just tell me where she is."

Tate takes in a deep breath and looks away at the wall.

"She went to a coffee shop to study on her lunch break. The one two blocks over is her favorite."

I nod and head toward the elevators.

"You're welcome."

I swear to God I hear her mumble, "Asshole," as I turn the corner.

I don't give a shit.

QUINN

I DIDN'T EXPECT to be so sad when I turned in my resignation letter, but I feel deflated, like a balloon after a date with a needle. I'm still struggling with what to say to Deacon and when to talk to him.

My dad was right. I do love him. I loved him the second we started dating, I just couldn't admit it to myself. I want to tell him, but I'm scared. Half of me loves him with every fiber in my body and wants to chase after him. The other half screams to cut my losses and go on with life.

I take a sip of coffee and flip through my study notes. I can't concentrate. About the time I decide to get up and leave, I glance toward the entrance.

This can't be happening.

Not now. I'm not ready.

Deacon walks through the door and damn near collides with a hipster. His jaw is set, and his eyes scan the room, until they land on me.

What the hell?

I've given him space. I sat around waiting for him to make a move and just say something. Anything. He's given me silence in return and now he wants to look at me like he's irritated?

"Were you going to tell me?" He marches toward me and looks down his nose, right into my eyes.

I blink a few times.

This is all wrong.

I was supposed to have time to prepare before I talked to him. "Deacon... I—"

"I've been working my ass off fixing that contract and I kept thinking, Quinn will come talk to me. Surely, she'll come to me and explain why she went behind my back and threw me under the bus to my brother and..." He stares out the window, unable to even look at me. "God, I don't even want to say her name, but *Tate* of all people. Instead you give me the cold shoulder and pretend like nothing happened." His eyes land on me once more and his voice rises a little more. "I was going to apologize for everything I said that day in the hall." His jaw ticks and everyone in the place stares at us, but he doesn't seem to care. "I didn't mean it. I didn't go anywhere with any girls. All I've done is work my ass off."

"Deacon, if you just—"

He cuts me off and talks over me, shaking his head. "Never took you for a quitter, though. I thought you were tough, all that stuff about earning everything you get. Thought maybe I meant something to you, but I guess I was wrong."

Tears form in the corners of my eyes and the back of my throat burns. "I've been wanting—"

"Just don't, Quinn. Save it for the next guy who loves you and break his heart."

I can't stop shaking. I want to say so many things, but he won't let me, and I'm not even sure they'd come out of my mouth if I wanted them to.

Deacon takes one final look at me and says, "Good luck with your law career."

He's already out the door before I can process what just happened. I don't even know what to think right now as I wipe my eyes and hurry to collect my things.

A barista comes over with some tissues. God, he's made me cry twice this week already. How could he possibly think any of this is my fault?

"Honey, are you okay?"

"I'm fine. Thanks." I gather my stuff in my arms and quietly slip out the door as fast as possible. He didn't even give me a chance to explain. Why would he think I would get him in trouble on purpose?

Then he basically says he loves me while insulting me at the same time.

You made the right decision. You don't need that in your life.

I curse the tears that won't stop coming and walk toward my car. Once I'm inside I call Heather. I need her more than anyone. "Hey." The word comes out as a croak.

"Everything okay? You sound sick."

"Everything is completely fucked."

"Want me to bury that son of a bitch? I totally know someone. Mafia guys come into the store all the time."

I can't even bring myself to laugh at her joke. "No. It's even worse because I don't want you to and I should."

"Are you good to drive?"

I sniffle. "Yeah. I'll be fine. I just need to breathe."

"Okay, well come over. I have wine and cheesecake. We can cry it out of your system."

"I'm getting in my car now."

"See you soon."

"Yeah." I hang up the phone and see the screensaver I snapped of Deacon and me when I was over at his place. Everything filters up through my chest again. I dump my books in the backseat and lay my head on the steering wheel and try to breathe.

Fuck being in love. It's the worst thing I've ever experienced.

DEACON

After the confrontation with Quinn, I came straight home. I couldn't go back to the office and stare at her, sitting at her desk, knowing I can't have her. She gave up, quit before we ever really began. In the beginning she always had one foot out the door, but it didn't feel that way toward the end.

I guess I should be thankful it ended now before I got even more serious about her. Who the fuck am I kidding? I've been serious about her since the first time I saw her. She's the only woman I've ever been serious about, that's ever made me feel something.

I knock back a drink and stare out at the skyline from my patio, wondering if things would have gone differently had I talked to her sooner.

It was two fucking days! Two days and she quits her job?

I'm a grown child and even I'm more mature than that. Another thing she and Tate always get wrong about me. I bet Tate isn't running off telling everyone how irresponsible and immature Quinn is.

I replay the situation from every scenario in my head, second-guessing every single decision I've made the past few days, including ambushing her at the coffee shop. Fuck, I was pretty mean to her. She deserved to know how I felt, but not like that.

That's the kind of shit that happens when you bury thirty years of emotional baggage and hide behind practical jokes. Finally find someone I care about, have a real connection to, and I sabotage the relationship.

Most of all, I can't stop thinking how good we were together. I was insane for her. Fuck. I still am. I don't know what to even do right now. It's like my skin itches everywhere and I don't know where to scratch.

I hear footsteps behind me and turn around half expecting to see Quinn even though I know there's no way in hell she'll show up here.

"The fuck you doing out here? Looks like you're about to have a mid-life crisis, buy a Harley, and marry a stripper." Dexter laughs.

"Look, I'm not really in the mood. So..."

"What the hell did you do to Quinn?"

"What?" My jaw ticks.

"I was in Decker's office and Tate busted in like Pontius Pilate, ready to crucify you. Decker kicked me out before I could hear the whole story. All I made out was something about a golf club and Quinn never came back from lunch."

"What the fuck does it matter? She quit."

Dexter shakes his head. "Sometimes I think you're a

bigger idiot than me. And sometimes you prove me right. Today is one of those days, bitch."

I stand up. "I said I'm not in the mood. Please don't make me be an asshole to you too."

He nods and takes a step toward the patio door. "You do realize it was a letter of resignation that doesn't take effect until after she graduates from school, right? She wasn't quitting anytime soon."

My eyes roam up to meet his, then I drop my head in my hands.

"You didn't know, did you?" Dexter takes a step into my apartment, then seems to change his mind and walks back out. "Decker just wanted it as a formality so he could look for someone to train alongside her. Shit even I knew that, and I don't pay attention to anything." He stares out at the lake in the distance. "The way you look, I'm guessing she's gone for real now, though."

"Fuck!" I beat my fist on the chair.

Looking up at Dexter, my chest heaves in huge waves, and I try to just breathe. My face has to be redder than hell, but I know losing my cool is what caused all my problems in the first place. It's not even anger, really. I just hate myself and it's hard to breathe. I think I might be having a panic attack.

She just makes me so damn crazy. All I want is her. It's the only thing I want in my life. I would give up everything for one more day with her. I want her so bad it physically hurts inside, an ache that runs bone-deep, everywhere at once.

"What'd you do?"

I scrub a hand over my face and pour myself another

drink. A tear slides down the side of my cheek and I freeze when it happens. It's something I've never felt before, not since I was a child anyway. I turn my head and wipe it away with my shoulder, so Dexter won't see. I've humiliated myself enough for one day. "I found her at the coffee shop."

"And?"

"You know those big machines that raze parking lots?"

"Jesus."

"It was a little like that. I couldn't stop myself. I was hurting so damn bad, man. I think subconsciously, I just wanted her to feel what I was feeling."

"Well, that's not good."

I don't know whether to laugh or hit him in the face for his nonchalant reaction. It's just how we talk to each other. Nothing is off limits from a good joke. "I made her cry. Not a single tear sliding down the cheek, either. Like, the floodgates opened, and she's tough as nails. Guarded. Called her a quitter, blamed her for ratting me out. Then I wished her luck with her career. I don't even think it was so much what I said to her, but how I said it." I shake my head. "Fuck, I even told her I loved her, but somehow twisted it into an insult in the same sentence. Like for her to save her bullshit for the next guy who loves her and crush his heart with it." I exhale, now even more ashamed than I was before. "There's no recovering from this. She's never going to speak to me again. *I* wouldn't speak to me again."

Dexter stares at me blankly for a while and pours a rocks glass for himself. He takes a long sip and groans. "Fuck me."

"What?"

"Are you a hundred percent sure you love her? That she's the one?"

My eyes narrow on him for even questioning my feelings for Quinn. "What the fuck do you think? Of course I'm crazy in love with her. What else would explain all that shit I told you? Does any of that sound like me?"

"No, actually. I've seen you take ass chewings from the meanest coaches in the country and just smile like you could do it all day." He sighs loudly. "Jesus. I mean, I could fix this for you. Quinn's such a great girl and could do so much better, though."

I start toward him and he laughs and holds his hands up in surrender.

"Look, I got you, man. You'll get her back. You just have to do every fucking thing I say, exactly how I say to do it."

I stand there, shaking my head, not even believing I'm considering whatever he's about to say. It's so absurd, and yet, at the same time I know I'd do anything for just ten more seconds with Quinn. "What exactly do you know about romance, Sir Fucksalot?"

He pretends to clutch his heart. "You wound me." He laughs. "I watch romance movies."

I snort. "Yeah. Okay. Whatever."

His face tightens. "I'm fucking serious. Haven't you ever had to watch chick flicks to get pussy? You know Netflix and chill stuff? Hallmark channel?"

"No way. I draw a hard line on girl movies. I can't handle them. Even the comedy ones suck."

"No wonder you can't keep a woman."

I roll my eyes.

"Okay, fine. It's whatever. I was just trying to help but if you don't need any…" He starts to walk off.

Before I know what I'm doing, I spin him back around by the forearm. "Let's not do anything hasty now. You have a plan or what?"

He pretends to brush some imaginary dirt off his sleeve where my fingers touched it. "Unlike you, I *do* watch those movies, and I pay attention to that shit, making notes in my head as I go along. In case I need to talk a chick into ass to mouth, dirty sanchez, the donkey punch, you know? The regular."

I shake my head at him.

"But to answer your question... yes. To fully understand, you have to grasp the big picture, then work out the details. You have to break down the romance into its basic structure. There's the meet-cute in the beginning. You know? Some over-the-top way in which the two people bump into each other that's a nearly impossible coincidence. Then they date for a while. That's when the first problem comes in. Something to throw a wrench into their lives to push them apart. They come back together. Another bigger problem pushes them apart. This repeats, amplifying in intensity, until the epic conflict arises, usually where the man does some shit that seems unforgiveable in the audience's eyes. Because the target audience is female, the guy has to be the problem. It's like a law of romance. He has to get on his knees and grovel to win her back. Women go insane for it." He pokes me with a finger. "And that's where *you* are right now."

I can't help but shake my head that he thinks about this

shit. I'd laugh if I wasn't so damn desperate. What's even worse is he's actually making some sense. "So how the fuck does he fix it? The guy in the movie?"

Dexter holds up his index finger and his eyes widen. "Ahh, this is the part I call the over-the-top redeeming gesture." He waggles his eyebrows.

"Well what the fuck does that entail?"

"Take a seat, rook. I'm gonna need some markers and a dry erase board to map out something spectacular after your epic fuck-up."

QUINN

I PULL out my study guide. It's Sunday, and it's been the longest week of my life. Four days have passed since Deacon ripped my heart out and stomped on it. I feel guilty for leaving everyone at the office hanging all week. It's not like me to not show up.

I managed to call Tate later on Wednesday, after the coffee shop incident, and told her I wasn't feeling well. She saw right through it, but she was nothing but kind and said she understood.

It's not even so much the words Deacon said but the way he looked at me. It was like he loved me and hated me at the same time.

I can't focus. I can't eat. I can't sleep.

Finally, I give up on studying and join Dad in the living room. He's watching the early football games.

I collapse on the couch. "The Bears play tonight?"

"Oh yeah. Primetime."

I don't get to ask who they're playing against because the doorbell rings. It's probably Heather coming to check on me. She invited me out last night, but I couldn't bring myself to get off the couch. Not yet, anyway. It's too soon, and last time I went out with her I ran into Deacon. I need a few days to mope around and feel sorry for myself, then I'll brush my shoulders off and get back to life. "I'll get it."

I open the door without bothering to check the peephole. I damn near have a heart attack as rage, humiliation, and then relief all wash over me within approximately two seconds. I blink and realize it's Dexter. "What the hell are you doing here?" The sound of a diesel engine lands in my ears. I move to look around him and see a white transport van parked out front. There's a small ramp lowering off the side for a wheelchair. I shake my head furiously, right at Dexter. "No." I wave a hand out at the van. "Whatever that is the answer is no."

I turn around to shut the door in his face, but he breezes past me like I'm not even there.

Ugh! Collins brothers!

"Mr. Richards, you've been watching games on this TV for far too long. That changes today." He tosses a Bears jersey in Dad's lap.

I stand in the hallway, dumbfounded, staring at the living room.

"You've got a brass set of balls showing up here, son!" Dad stares at Dexter for a second. "Who the fuck is this clown, Quinn? He looks just like Deacon, but it ain't him."

Dexter doesn't miss a beat, like he's a high-pressure marketer. "I'm the goddamn clown who's going to make all your dreams come true today, sir." Dexter pulls tickets from his pocket and fans them out in front of Dad.

Dad's eyes go wide. Fast. "Well okay then. Tell me more." He looks over at me and shrugs, then points at Dexter. "I mean, he's not Deacon."

This is going downhill fast, past the point of recovery. I might as well just not even be here.

Dexter looks like he's on *The Price is Right*, rattling off a prize package. "Well, tell me how this sounds, sir." He pauses to flash a smile right at me, and I swear to God his tooth sparkles.

I have to be in a dream right now. This can't be happening.

"Tailgating on the upper level of the Waldron Deck. You'll hang out with Mike Ditka and Brian Urlacher for one hour. We'll float a keg together then have a meal at The Chicago Firehouse Restaurant. Followed with a VIP suite to watch the game."

I know Deacon put him up to this but why? The things he said to me at the coffee shop made it sound pretty final. Why the hell is he going out of his way for my dad?

None of this makes sense.

"I know it sounds amazing, Dad, but there's no way you can handle all that." I hate to crush my old man's heart but it's true.

"No worries." Dexter smirks at me. "Sir, I have a nurse waiting outside with a fully handicap-accessible van to provide you with transportation and healthcare should the need arise." He leans down to Dad and whispers something, but then holds his hands out in front of his chest suggesting the nurse may be well endowed too.

These assholes thought of everything.

Dexter walks over to the window near Dad and pulls

back the curtain. Dad leans forward slightly and sees the same thing I do. There's a blonde girl dressed in tight jeans with a Bears jersey tied up at her waist showing off her midriff.

I pull Dexter back by the collar. "That's Abigail from the Dallas office." I hiss the words at him.

He shrugs. "She went to nursing school for a semester. It's totally fine and she's hot. Look how happy he is. Don't be a dick. You're ruining his moment."

I scowl at him. He thinks I'm being a dick. He came over here and got my dad all excited about this game.

Dad stares at Abigail then looks back at me, raises his eyebrows, and says, "Oh, we're going to have some fun today, baby girl."

"Excellent choice, Mr. Richards. Please allow me." Dexter moves past me and grabs the back of his wheelchair.

Dad pats him on the arm as they head to the door. "You may just be my new best friend."

Dexter looks back at me and says, "You comin'?"

I sigh and grab my bag. It's not like they're giving me much of a choice. There's no way in hell I'm turning Dexter loose with my dad for the whole day.

The driver loads Dad into the van, and I yank Dexter back by the sleeve of his shirt. "I know Deacon put you up to this and it's not going to work. Even if you get my dad to the game and he has the time of his life..." My heart stutters in my chest when Dexter smirks at me. He looks so much like Deacon it's painful to see his smile.

Dexter puts his palms on my cheeks, and I wonder what the hell he's doing until he pinches both of them and grins wider. "Well, aren't you adorable. I see why Deacon likes you. But guess what?"

"What?" I put both hands on my hips, but I can't even look at him.

"It's already working."

My confidence falters a little as he steps away. I inhale a deep breath and get my shit together. God, every one of those brothers is so damn cocky. We'll see if it works.

Before Dexter can climb in, I tap him on the shoulder, less forceful this time around.

He spins around but doesn't look annoyed. "What's up?"

I look down at the ground because I don't want him to see the shame I know is plastered to my face. "Is he going to be there?"

Dexter puts a hand on my shoulder, and I'll be damned if he doesn't actually look sincere this time. "When the time is right. Not before."

I nod and climb into the van. Dad's smiling so big it's kind of contagious. It's freaking impossible to be upset when he's having possibly the greatest day of his life.

Abigail has her paws all over him, helping him get his jersey on.

Dad's in heaven and it feels like a little piece of my heart might have stitched itself back together.

———

DEXTER LIVES UP to his word. The day has been amazing so far. Dad got to hang out with Mike Ditka and Brian Urlacher, and they talked football the entire hour. They didn't even act embarrassed at all Dad's questions. They all just sat there like they've been friends their entire lives.

We had great food. God, the food was incredible. It hits me in the chest how much Dad needed this, and I've never had the time or the financial support to do it for him.

Deacon made this happen. He did this for me. It means more to me than he'll ever know, and my heart feels like it's slowly coming back together again, because he really does pay attention to every little detail and knows every little gear and pulley that makes me tick. I know somewhere in my heart I have it in me to forgive him, but I'm still not sold on the idea. He hurt me so bad, even thinking about him right now is painful. If I just give in, what kind of precedent does that set for any possible relationship? That he can just walk all over me when he feels like it, then stroll through the front door the next day?

No, he needs to beg and plead. I need to look in his eyes and see if he's sincere or not.

All the same, I glance around, missing him more than ever and wishing he was here and things between us were okay again.

It pains me to say it, but Dexter was right. Their plan is working, slowly but surely. This morning I wouldn't have given Deacon the time of day, and now I already find myself willing to hear him out.

Stupid men!

Now, we're up in the VIP suite. Dad's drinking non-alcoholic beer because of his medications but he doesn't mind. He's doing what he loves. He's living again, and I have to bite back the emotions swirling inside me.

"Enjoying yourself?" Dexter nudges up against me.

"Okay. I'll admit, this is incredible. Thank you so much for making him happy." I gesture toward Dad.

Dexter shrugs. "Don't mention it. It's nothing. We do it every Sunday when there's a home game. He's always welcome."

Several seconds pass between us and I twiddle my thumbs. "Where is he?" The question comes out before I can stop it.

Dexter turns. "He didn't want to cause a scene or interrupt you and your Dad having a great time. He only cares that you two enjoy yourselves and he thought that might not happen if he showed up. He knows between the medical condition and work, school..." He pauses. "Shit. Sorry, he told me about law school."

I shrug. "It doesn't matter now. I'm sure he needed someone to talk to and it sounds like you were it. Which makes sense, twins and all that, right?"

Dexter nods. "Anyway, he knows you guys don't get to go out and do stuff like this. Believe it or not, it's not just some thing to win you back. His number one priority today is for you and your dad to have the best day ever. That's all he cares about right now. I'm sure you guys have a ton of shit to work out, but it can wait."

I wrap my arms around my center and wish Deacon was here so I could at least thank him.

"Stop overthinking this. Let your hair down and pretend you like football. Here, have a beer." He hands me a bottle.

I try to do what he says and just enjoy this day for what it is and relax, but I can't just turn off the way I feel like that. There's no on and off switch.

Dexter grins. "I'm not normally this nice, so you could at least pretend to enjoy hanging out with me too."

"Yeah, yeah." I clink my bottle with his and take a big sip.

It does taste really good. I walk over to Dad, put my arm around his neck, and give him a gentle squeeze. "You having the best time ever or what?"

"Yeah, kiddo. I am."

"Me too."

I'm so in love with Deacon, but I just don't know what to do. One question lingers at the back of my mind.

Is he doing this out of guilt or because he wants to make this work?

DEACON

I'VE HUNG back at a safe distance all day watching Quinn and her dad. There were a few moments where I swore she was looking around, trying to spot me. Maybe that's wishful thinking on my part, but I'm going to believe it's true.

It was damn near impossible not to run to her, wrap her in my arms, beg for her forgiveness, and tell her everything would be okay. I know it's just my mind playing tricks on me. I doubt this plan has a single fucking chance of working after the way I treated her, but once Dexter told me his general idea—*"Give Quinn the best day of her life without you there."*—I knew exactly what to do.

I didn't even have to think twice. Even if she doesn't take me back, I want her and her dad to have the best day ever. They deserve it after all the shit they've been through. This won't be the last, either. Just like the flowers every Friday, I'll never stop doing nice things for her.

I don't want Quinn to work anywhere else. She belongs

with me, every fucking day. I want to go to work with her and go home with her. We'll have the American dream. She'll move in with me, we'll get married, and start making babies, if that's what she wants. If she doesn't want kids, I'll get a damn vasectomy. I don't give a shit. I just want to give her everything she wants for the rest of our lives.

I can see it all so vividly inside my head. Nothing will feel right again if Quinn doesn't take me back. Nothing will matter if I don't have her to share it with.

I'm not very religious but fuck me if I haven't been saying silent prayers all damn day, making God all kinds of impossible promises I probably couldn't live up to, if I could just get her back.

The fourth quarter ends but they haven't left the suite yet. It's time to make my move. My hands tremble like a rookie at the Super Bowl and my palms clam up. I played football at some of the highest levels possible and never got nervous, but now, I'm about to die.

The stakes have never been higher in my life. Because it's my future on the line. I can't live without her.

It's now or never with Quinn and I can't live with never. I walk to the entrance and give Dex the signal he came up with. I scratch my nose with my middle finger and roll my eyes at the same time.

He makes a circle with his index finger and thumb on his leg, then laughs when I look at it, because he'll get to punch me in the arm later. He taps Abigail on the shoulder, and she wheels Mr. Richards toward the exit. After that, Dex smiles and actually gives me a thumbs up.

Maybe he has a heart after all.

Quinn hasn't noticed me yet. I hear her voice call out from inside the room. "Where the hell are you taking him now?"

"After party with the players. Dad's gonna be up late tonight. Don't worry. He's in good hands."

I'm standing right outside the door as they wheel him out.

Abigail and Mr. Richards stop next to me.

I hold out my hand. "Hope you had a good time today, sir."

"Yes, I did." He holds his hand out, but scowls at me. He motions for me to lean down and I do. He grits in my ear, mustering up the most menacing tone he can, "Tread lightly. Hurt my daughter again and you'll lose a knee. We understand each other?"

"Yes, sir."

He straightens up and grins, like that's all taken care of. "All right, then. If you'll excuse me, this pretty lady is taking me to a party."

Dex gives me a fist bump as he follows them out.

I step inside just as Quinn starts toward the door. She freezes in place and her face pales. Fuck, she looks like she's about to cry, and I think my heart shatters into a million pieces, just watching her about to crumble.

Without hesitation, I run toward her, afraid she's about to break down.

She holds up a hand before I get there and I stop in my tracks, holding my hands up.

"Sorry, I just, you looked…"

"It's okay."

I hook a thumb over my shoulder. "Look, I can go. It just seemed like…"

She shakes her head. "No, it's okay. Now is good."

"Look, Quinn, I've tried to think of the right things to say all day long. How, I mean what… God, this is hard. Just, nothing seemed good enough. I don't think there are any words that are good enough."

She stares down at the floor and I think it's because she's about to cry and doesn't want me to see.

Fuck, I'm ruining this.

"Quinn, please, can you look at me?" Then, I feel it again, a fucking tear running down *my* cheek. I don't try to hide it, though. I don't try to push all the hurt back inside, because I don't give a shit what anyone else thinks. I want her to know that seeing her in pain, pain that I caused, is the most excruciating experience of my life.

Her head tilts up and her eyes land on my cheek.

My voice starts to crack as I speak. "I-I'm sorry."

Her face is pink, and I can't tell if her tears are angry or if she's just hurt.

"I overreacted. I just… I could rattle off a thousand excuses about shit, but I won't. I don't want to make any excuses. I've never done anything like that in my life. It's not who I am, and I am truly sorry that I put you through that and humiliated you the way I did."

"I would never go behind your back, Deacon." She wipes a tear from her eye. "I was at my desk talking to Tate when Beckley called. She was standing right there when I pulled up the contract. There was nothing I could do. I didn't even realize you were the one who handled it until Decker pulled you into the conference room. You hurt me, Deacon. Crushed me. You broke my heart."

It's hard to look her in the eyes because I'm so ashamed, but I don't dare look away because I deserve every bit of the pain. "I'm sorry. I'll do whatever it takes. If you don't want anything to do with me, I understand, and I'll stay away. I just want you to be happy, even if that doesn't include me." I sniff again. "It will be absolute hell. Torture, even. But I'll leave you alone." Then, I do something I never thought I'd do in my entire life. It's like my body has a mind of its own. I fall down on my knees in front of her.

Her eyes widen.

"I'm begging you, though. Please. I want another chance. It doesn't have to be today, or tomorrow, or even a month from now. If you'll just promise to give me one more chance, I swear I will make it up to you a thousand times over. I've never begged in my life, never asked anyone for anything, but a sliver of hope with you is worth a lifetime of begging."

Her eyes soften a hint and more tears flow down her cheeks.

I want nothing more than to wrap her in my arms and kiss her so hard she's dizzy, but I can't. Not anymore. I gaze up at her green eyes and it's hard not to get lost in them. "I love you, Quinn. I've been in love with you for a long time. As long as I've been sending you flowers. I should've told you sooner."

Her eyes narrow. "Don't say things you don't mean, Deacon. We were just a fling back then."

"No." I shake my head. "I loved you the first time I

saw you. I know it sounds ridiculous, but it's the truth. I knew the only way you'd give me any type of chance was if it was casual. I know what you thought of me, my reputation, but you're the only woman I've been with since you started at the firm. That's where the closet came in. I've learned every detail I could about you from the beginning, and I loved you so damn hard the whole time. I was just too scared to tell you, because I thought I'd run you off. I used sex as a reason just to be near you because you kept turning me down and throwing the flowers away. But I didn't give up then, and I won't give up now. I fucked up. I know that. It won't happen again. You're it for me, just let me prove it to you. The only way you're getting rid of me is if you tell me to leave you alone. And the only reason I'd leave you alone then, is because I love you so fucking much, and I never want to see you hurting because of something I did."

Tears stream down her cheeks, and I want nothing more than to just wipe them away, just hold her and promise over and over this will never happen again.

"I love you too, Deacon. I just…"

I rise to my feet. She said the words I've waited a lifetime to hear.

I hold my arms out, letting her make the decision for herself. I don't want to force anything on her this time. I want it to be purely her decision. "Come back to me, please. Quinn, I'm nothing without you."

She stands there for a moment, staring at my outstretched arms.

Tears slide down her cheeks, then she rushes into me, burying her face in my chest.

I wrap her up in a hug and squeeze her against me so hard I worry she might not be able to breathe. "Thank God." I look down at her. "Thank God." I drop a kiss on top of her hair and run a hand up and down her back.

Just feeling her up against me, her heart thudding against my ribs, everything in life is perfect again, even if it's only for a moment. I just sit there and hold her, praying it never ends. Praying that it's real.

Finally, her chin tilts up and she looks at me once more, only this time there's a smile on her face. "Hi."

"Hi." I lean down and kiss her, because it just feels like the right thing to do. Everything clicks. The moment our lips touch, heat blooms in my chest again and colors grow vibrant. That feeling of floating on the clouds returns.

We continue to kiss, like two old souls reunited after decades. That's what it feels like, even though it's only been a few days.

"I need you so damn bad." I whisper the words against her neck, backing her up to the glass of the suite window that overlooks the Soldier Field. "Need you in my life. I can't fucking breathe without you."

"I need you too, Deacon." This time Quinn is the one who kisses me.

It turns passionate quickly, her needy hands roaming my chest.

I grab her by each wrist and pin them above her head on the glass, then rake my eyes up and down her body as her chest heaves with deep, labored breaths. When my mouth hits her ear, I whisper, "You have no idea how bad I want you. Right here. Right now. But we need to go spend time with your dad at the party. And it's too soon. When

I'm with you I want to move at the speed of light, but I know going slow is better for us."

Quinn's eyebrows rise. "You're turning down sex with me, again, at Soldier Field, to go hang out with my dad?"

"Well…" My eyes narrow on her. "I have one thing I could do that would be acceptable."

"What's that?"

"A proper apology."

Quinn stares at me like I'm an alien from another planet. "Isn't that, like, what all this was?"

"I said a proper apology, Quinn." I flip her around and press her up against the glass.

"Ohh."

My mouth is right in her ear. "One that's tailored specifically for your own benefit."

"Well, I do like the sound of that."

I reach around and unbutton her jeans, then yank them down to the floor. "An apology that leaves my balls aching all night as punishment."

"Tell me more, sir."

I pull her panties down to the floor and she steps out of them and her jeans. "It requires a demonstration."

I bend down and shove her panties in my pocket. Some traditions must continue. I rise and cup her pussy in my hand. "So. Fucking. Wet."

Quinn's mouth moves to say something, and I slide a finger in. It turns her sentence into a soft moan. There's something about watching her squirm and writhe under my touch that just does it for me, every single time. She's like an instrument I've already mastered. I love playing it more than anything in the world and can't wait to perform the rest of my life.

I lower myself to my knees behind her, spread her ass, and sit back on my heels, just to stare at her slick, glistening folds. "I need to work fast, since we have somewhere to be."

Quinn nods.

I always love doing the opposite of what she thinks, catching her by surprise. So, I slowly kiss up the backs of her legs, all the way to the bottom of her ass. I take my time working to her inner thighs, teasing closer and closer to where she needs my mouth. She tries to push back into me, but I have my hands on her ass and keep her from getting what she wants.

"Thought you were going to be fast." Her words come out on several pants.

Teasing her is the best part. "Don't rush an artist."

"So damn cocky."

I grin, my mouth just inches from her pussy, wanting to taste it more than anything in the world. I plan to work fast, when the time is right, but amping her up with anticipation is vital to the process. It has to be a slow build to the crescendo.

My tongue darts out and grazes her clit. It sends a shudder down the back of her legs.

That's right.

I slide my thumb down and work lazy circles around it while I take my tongue as deep as it will go. One of her hands flies back and paws at the side of my head, looking for anything to grab hold of. She's already so close, I can feel it in the tiny vibrations of her body. Before long, I have two fingers teasing the secret spot deep inside her while my tongue flicks across her clit.

"God, Deacon." Her fingernails dig into my scalp and she pulls my face into her as she releases. Her thighs tremble and there's no better feeling in the world than satisfying her, giving her exactly what she needs when she needs it.

Her hips buck and she jolts a few more times, then her muscles relax. I slowly work her jeans back up around her waist and button them in the front, kissing up the side of her neck as I do it.

"My panties?"

I love it when she's so worn out she speaks in sentence fragments. "They belong to me, just like you."

Quinn falls back into my arms and shakes her head, both of us staring out at the field. "I can't believe you did all this for us."

"I can't take all the credit. It was Dexter's idea."

"I know. He told me."

I spin her around to face me. "Of course he did." I snicker.

"It's not like that. Believe it or not, he was sweet and told me you thought of all the details. He just shoved you in the right direction."

"He watches romantic comedies."

We both laugh.

"Really?"

"He claims it's to get laid, but I think he watches them alone at night eating ice cream."

Quinn shakes her head. "Who would've thought…"

"So did it work?" I grin to lighten the mood, but inside

I'm trembling in equal parts anticipation and fear of her response.

She smacks at my shoulder. "Yeah, dickhead. It worked. You got the girl." She leans up on her tiptoes bringing her mouth to mine for a soft kiss. "Just don't ever put me through that again. Promise?"

There's not a doubt in my mind. I will never lose her again. "I promise."

EPILOGUE

Quinn

"I'm so proud of you." Deacon opens the car door and ushers me into the passenger seat. "Time to celebrate. I made reservations."

"Okay." I smirk and buckle my seatbelt as he goes around to the driver's side. "Where you taking me?"

"It's a surprise." He starts up the car and backs out of his parking space.

"I have a surprise for you too."

"Oh yeah? What is it?"

"If I told you, I'd have to kill you."

"You've been watching too many action movies with your dad."

"You're one to talk. I heard the two of you up late last weekend."

"Guilty. We were watching porn, though."

"Deacon Collins!" I smack his arm and laugh at the same time.

Some things never change.

"We were studying the cinematography. It was incredible. You should've seen the lighting, and they got this one shot…"

"Just stop before you dig yourself a hole."

Deacon puts his hands up in mock surrender, holding back a laugh.

It took some convincing to get Dad to move in with us. He pleaded for us to put him in assisted living when I told him I was moving in with Deacon, but neither one of us were having that. Deacon goes out of his way to spend time with him. They watched sports nonstop while I studied for finals and I'm sure it'll continue as I study for the bar.

We go to all the Bears home games and Deacon is slowly teaching me everything he knows about football. I usually fall asleep while Dad sits there absorbing every little detail of Deacon's stories.

He had his place completely renovated to accommodate Dad. Everything is handicap accessible, and Dad can nearly function on his own when we aren't there.

Sometimes it doesn't even seem real, that I'm with him.

"You going to at least give me a hint?"

I can't keep it in any longer. I'm about to burst at the seams. "I wanted to discuss a career choice with you."

"Oh yeah?" His knuckles grip the steering wheel a little tighter, but he doesn't overreact and keeps a smile plastered to his face.

"Yeah. I think it's best for all of us if I stay at The Hunter Group. What are your thoughts?" I watch his reaction in my peripheral vision.

"Seriously? Don't toy with me, woman."

"Yeah, I want to end where I started."

"That makes me so damn happy." He pulls into a parking space near the restaurant. Before we exit the car, Deacon takes my hand and leans across the console. "You won't regret it. I promise."

"I know." I touch his face then kiss his lips.

"Mmm." He leans back and gazes into my eyes. "Come on we better get inside before I bend you over the hood of my car."

Deacon leads me through the front door and the moment we enter the dining room everyone from work jumps out and yells, "Surprise!" There's a huge banner that reads CONGRATULATIONS, QUINN.

"What is this?"

He cocks an eyebrow up at me. "I don't know. A center for ants? What's it look like?"

I shake my head. "Point taken." I give him a huge hug, then move through the room to thank everyone for coming.

Even when we're separated, I can't stop craning my neck back to smile at him, though. It's hard to take my eyes off the man I love.

EPILOGUE

Deacon

I stand next to Quinn, watching her scan the room. I know who she's looking for and there's no way I wouldn't make sure he's here. When she doesn't see him, her smile fades.

I whisper in her ear, "I have another surprise for you." I nod to Abigail and she walks through a side door and then returns, wheeling in Mr. Richards.

"Dad!" She sprints over to him.

I walk behind, slowly soaking up the moment and taking videos and pictures with my phone, so she'll have them later.

"I'm so damn proud of you, kiddo."

She bends down and gives him a kiss on the cheek. "I love you."

He shoots me a wink and we all make our way to the huge table in the middle of the room. Over the course of the evening, everyone takes turns going around telling stories about how Quinn has bailed them out of a jam or gone above and beyond at work. Her Dad grins the entire time, loving the praise being heaped on his daughter. The goal was to have her feel like she was on top of the world and I'm positive I've succeeded.

"I think I speak for everyone when I say we wouldn't know our heads from our asses without you, Quinn." Tate raises her glass.

"That's exactly right. I'd be completely lost without you and I know you'll be just as effective as an attorney. So proud that you'll be one of ours." Decker winks at her.

When we arrived earlier, I told him she was staying at the firm.

"Quinn, you definitely keep my brothers in check." Donavan grins his ass off, like she doesn't save his ass as much as anybody's, but it's clear he's joking.

"Quinn, I know all about your secret stash of pens and office supplies." Dex laughs and Abigail smacks the back of his head, Gibbs-style. "Ow! Damn. Okay. You're awesome, Quinn. Thanks for everything." He grins and nods to me. "Your turn, big boy."

There's just one more thing that will make today perfect.

I scoot my chair back and hold my hand out to her.

"Umm. Okay. What's this?" She takes my hand and rises from her seat. "What are you doing?"

The confusion on her face makes this so much better. I walk over to her dad and hold out my hand. He smiles as he reaches into his pocket and pulls out a black box.

I turn back to Quinn. I'm doing this the right way. Like in the romance movies I've watched with her. Clearly that shit works, and I want every tool in my arsenal to make Quinn happy the rest of her life. I stare deeply into the same green eyes I fell in love with the first time I saw them, knowing without a doubt she's the one.

I take her left hand in mine and drop to a knee.

"Quinn, you're the most beautiful woman I've ever met, inside and out. The first time I saw you, I knew. I can't explain how or why, I just felt it in every cell of my body. And I want to tell you something in front of everyone tonight." I look back over my shoulder at my brothers and our closest friends.

Tate, who never cries, dabs a napkin at the corner of her eyes.

"Words don't exist to accurately express how much I love you. You're my best friend. Every morning, when I wake up next to you, I feel like the luckiest man alive. But there's one thing missing. A promise that you'll be mine forever. So, I'm lowering myself before you today to ask you one question. Will you marry me?"

Her head bobs up and down. "Yes, Deacon. Yes! A thousand times yes!" Her entire body trembles as she leans down to kiss me.

I slide the ring on her finger. It's an emerald-green princess cut that matches her eyes.

"I love you so much. I had no idea you were going to do this." Her eyes keep darting from the ring then back to me. The largest smile I've ever seen spreads across her face.

She's absolutely glowing, and I plan to work my ass off every day to keep it that way.

When our moment is over, everyone makes their

rounds congratulating us.

I look at Dex and Donavan, wondering which poor bastard will be next, now that Decker and I are off the market.

Once everyone has told us how happy they are for us, I take Quinn's hands in mine and just stare into her eyes. "Fiancée."

"Fiancé." She does a little fancy curtsy and we both laugh.

I take her in my arms and hold her close to me, never wanting to let go. I kiss her forehead, then pull her back to me once more.

I can't think of anything in the world better than this moment, right here, right now, and I know the future will only be better.

Because she's all mine.

Thank you so much for reading Bossy Playboy! I hope you loved it! We have a BONUS epilogue for you!

Give me my BONUS epilogue!

Grab the first four books in the series with just ONE CLICK!

Filthy Playboy is next! Come meet Dexter and Abigail.

Also by Alex Wolf

Want to learn more about where it all started with Weston and the Hunter Group? Tap on the picture above!

COCKY SUITS BOXSET

Damon

Naughty Girl

Rock God

Guitar God

A Bad Boy for Christmas

Shagged

Professor's Pet

ABOUT ALEX WOLF

Alex hails from the Midwest and currently resides in Tampa, Florida with his girlfriend Chelle, his son and two cats. His daughter is currently serving in the U.S. Navy. He's a huge fan of THE Ohio State Buckeyes and the Cleveland Browns.

O-H…

He enjoys writing steamy romance but more importantly he enjoys the "research" required to produce the steamy scenes. If you like filthy-mouthed, possessive alpha heroes and steamy romance, then he's the author for you!

Join my PRIVATE facebook group!
Join Alex Wolf's Den

Sign up for my newsletter and be the first to know about future releases!
Sign me up!

Where you can follow me

.

Printed in Great Britain
by Amazon

15216210R00171